The Pain Behind The Pole

The Pain Behind The Pole, Volume 1

Sent

Published by Dynasty Publications, 2024.

THE PAIN BEHIND THE POLE

First edition. July 18, 2024.

ISBN: 979-8227991430

Written by Sent.

Table of Contents

Chapter 1: Echoes of Atlanta Dreams.................................1

Chapter 2: Zy's Enigmatic Dance 6

Chapter 3: Beneath the Surface.................................12

Chapter 4: Dancing on the Edge.................................16

Chapter 5: The Charismatic Arrival of Renz.........................27

Chapter 6: Whispers of Desire 35

Chapter 7: Shadows of Love and Deceit 39

Chapter 8: Debts in the Shadows.................................45

Chapter 9: Get It How You Live.................................50

Chapter 10: Miami Nights.................................63

Chapter 11: In the Eye of the Storm.................................76

Chapter 12: Symphony of Shottas.................................86

Chapter 13: An Awakening.................................91

Chapter 14: Trail of Tears.................................97

All Praise To The Most High!

Dedicated To Everyone Who Left. They Left Me For Dead, Yet I've Never Felt More Alive. What Was Designed To Break Me Only Made Me Stronger

For Every Young Woman Who Attempted To Use The Pole And Her Body As A Viable Means To Transcend The Confines Of Their Oppressing Situations This One's For You.

Chapter 1: Echoes of Atlanta Dreams

In the crisp August of 2023, Tachelle Emani Davis stepped off the Greyhound bus, her excitement palpable amidst the warm breeze that whispered promises of new beginnings. At 4'10", Tachelle's voluptuous frame, weighing 145 pounds, moved gracefully through the bustling streets. Her mahogany skin, with red undertones, gleamed under the summer sun, complemented by her short, twisted dreadlocks and light hazel, cat-like eyes that lent her an exotic touch.

Dressed in her favorite faded denim jacket and a floral summer dress, Tachelle embraced her optimistic yet shy demeanor. Determined to succeed, she carried the weight of her insecurities, a small stomach pudge and meaty thighs, from her rural roots in Mississippi to the new big city. The challenge of her condominium's rent loomed as Tachelle unpacked her bags. The gold-colored, beat-up Honda Accord, a testament to her journey, awaited in the parking lot. Raggedy in appearance but resilient in spirit, it symbolized the dreamer's transition from a small town to the vast cityscape.

With textbooks in hand and a heart full of dreams, Tachelle navigated the vibrant campus of Clark Atlanta University. Inside Professor Eleanor Brooks' classroom, the air buzzed with anticipation. Tachelle, a county girl in a new big city, found herself amidst an eclectic mix of students, her eyes sparkling with both excitement and a hint of shyness.

Professor Brooks, a tall, slender woman with silver-streaked hair and piercing blue eyes, spoke with an authority that commanded attention. Her tailored suits and immaculate posture exuded confidence and wisdom. As she addressed the eager students, her voice carried a warmth that belied her strict demeanor. "August marks not only the beginning of a new semester but a journey of discovery. Atlanta holds challenges, my dear students, but within them lie your greatest lessons."

As Tachelle absorbed the wisdom, the city's summer energy wrapped around her like a warm embrace. Little did she know, the city's rhythm, the promise of newfound friendships, and the shadows of unforeseen challenges awaited her as she embarked on the tale of her Atlanta dreams.

The August sun cast a golden hue over the city as Tachelle, guided by Professor Brooks' words, embarked on the journey through her first semester. Her floral summer dress swayed with each step, a vibrant contrast to the urban landscape. The weather, warm and inviting, seemed to mirror the optimism that fueled Tachelle's spirit.

As she navigated the city streets, the distant hum of conversations and the rhythmic beats of street musicians surrounded her. Tachelle found herself enchanted by the kaleidoscope of people and cultures that Atlanta embraced. The season's energy pulsed through the air, a mix of anticipation and the buzz of city life.

She stumbled upon a street market filled with vendors selling an array of goods, from handmade jewelry to fresh produce. The aroma of food trucks wafted through the air, and Tachelle's stomach grumbled. She approached a taco truck and ordered a plate of spicy chicken tacos.

"First time in Atlanta?" the vendor, a middle-aged man with a friendly smile, asked as he handed her the plate.

"Yeah, just got here," Tachelle replied, her eyes wide with wonder.

"Well, welcome! Atlanta's a big city with a big heart. You'll love it here," he assured her.

As Tachelle continued to explore, she noticed a girl about her age standing by a boutique window, admiring a display of vintage dresses. Her tall, slender frame and striking features were impossible to miss. She wore a white and gold Versace jean couture outfit, and her curly hair bounced with each movement.

Tachelle felt a mixture of admiration and intimidation. She gathered her courage and approached the girl. "Hi, I'm Tachelle. I couldn't help but notice your outfit. It's stunning."

The girl turned and flashed a radiant smile. "Thank you! I'm Zy. Nice to meet you, Tachelle. Just moved here?"

"Yeah, from Mississippi. It's a bit overwhelming, but I'm excited," Tachelle admitted.

"Darling, this city is a dance floor, and we're just learning the steps," Zy proclaimed, her graceful movements emphasizing the rhythm of their newfound friendship. Tachelle, still adjusting to the vibrant beat of Atlanta, followed Zy's lead with a mix of awe and excitement.

Their explorations took them to hidden corners of the city, where the summer blooms adorned the streets. Tachelle marveled at the diverse fashion statements, from trendy streetwear to bohemian ensembles that painted the city with an artistic flair. Zy's couture outfit became a beacon of style amid the kaleidoscope of Atlanta's fashion scene.

The duo ventured into quaint bookshops and lively jazz bars, where the music resonated with the heartbeat of the city. Each scene unfolded like a chapter in Tachelle's story, a tapestry of experiences woven with the threads of summer's warmth and the vibrant hues of the city's personality.

One evening, they found themselves at a cozy jazz bar called "The Blue Note." The dimly lit room was filled with the soulful sounds of a saxophone, and the walls were adorned with photos of legendary jazz musicians. Tachelle and Zy sat at a small table near the stage, sipping on cocktails and soaking in the atmosphere.

"This place is amazing," Tachelle said, her eyes closed as she swayed to the music.

"It is. Atlanta has so much to offer. You just have to be open to it," Zy replied, her eyes twinkling with excitement.

Amid the adventures, Tachelle's gold Honda, though beat-up and raggedy, became a reliable companion on the urban canvas. Its rumbling engine echoed the determination that propelled her forward, each journey a testament to her resilience.

One vivid scene unfolded inside Professor Brooks' classroom, where the hum of discussions blended with the professor's insightful lectures. Tachelle, slightly insecure about her small stomach pudge and meaty thighs, found solace in the academic sanctuary, where dreams and lessons intertwined.

As the sun dipped below the Atlanta skyline, casting a warm glow over the city, Tachelle and Zy continued their dance through the summer evening. Little did Tachelle know that the echoes of her Atlanta dreams would soon transform into a tale of unexpected challenges and newfound strength in the chapters that awaited her.

As the weeks went by, Tachelle found herself growing more confident. Her friendship with Zy deepened, and she began to form connections with other students as well. There was Marcus, a charismatic business major with a passion for entrepreneurship, and Leila, a bubbly art student who always had a sketchbook in hand.

One afternoon, as Tachelle and Zy lounged in the grassy quad, Marcus and Leila joined them. The group chatted and laughed, their camaraderie a testament to the bonds they were forming.

"So, Tachelle, what brings you to Atlanta?" Marcus asked, his curiosity genuine.

"I needed a change. I wanted to experience something different, something bigger than my small town," Tachelle explained.

"Well, you've definitely come to the right place. Atlanta has a way of pushing you to grow," Leila added, her eyes sparkling with enthusiasm.

As the sun set and the city lights began to twinkle, Tachelle felt a sense of belonging she hadn't anticipated. The challenges of adjusting to a new city were still there, but with friends like Zy, Marcus, and Leila by her side, she felt ready to face them.

The echoes of her Atlanta dreams resonated within her, a symphony of hope and determination. Tachelle knew that her journey was just beginning, and with each step she took, she was forging her path in this vibrant, sprawling city.

Chapter 2: Zy's Enigmatic Dance

The sun dipped below the Atlanta skyline, painting the city in hues of twilight as Tachelle and Zy continued their exploration. The city, now adorned with the soft glow of streetlights, seemed to hold secrets waiting to be unveiled.

As they strolled through the urban landscape, Zy's Versace ensemble sparkled like city lights against the evening sky. Tachelle, feeling a mixture of awe and apprehension, took in the striking contrast between her own modest attire and Zy's runway-worthy presence. Zy, with her long, nearly twisted dreadlocks that hung gracefully, exuded an air of confidence and grace. Her diva-ish aura remained intact, commanding attention as they entered the heart of the city's nightlife.

The night was alive with the sounds of laughter, music, and the distant hum of city life. Zy led Tachelle to a hidden gem known as "Starlight Lounge," a renowned spot where Atlanta's diverse beats converged. The entrance, adorned with a gold-plated sign, welcomed them into a realm of shimmering lights and rhythmic melodies.

Inside, the ambiance was electric. The dance floor pulsed with energy as bodies moved in perfect synchrony to the music. Zy, ever the confident guide, beckoned Tachelle to join the dance. Despite her shy demeanor, Tachelle found herself caught in the rhythm, her movements reflecting the city's heartbeat.

As they danced, Tachelle noticed the eclectic crowd – a mix of artists, students, and professionals, all converging in a harmonious celebration of life. The air was filled with a mélange of fragrances – perfumes, colognes, and the tantalizing aroma of exotic cuisines from the lounge's kitchen.

Zy, with her infectious enthusiasm, introduced Tachelle to Malik "Charmz" Davis, a charismatic dancer with a magnetic stage presence. Malik's denim jacket and effortlessly cool demeanor embodied the free spirit of Atlanta's artistic community.

"Hey there, Tachelle! Zy tells me you're the fresh breeze from Mississippi. Welcome to the A!" Malik's voice was smooth, his words a blend of street poetry and Southern charm. He extended a hand, and Tachelle, still catching her breath from the dance, felt an immediate connection.

"Nice to meet you, Charmz. Atlanta's wilder than I expected," Tachelle admitted, a slight smile playing on her lips.

Malik chuckled. "Girl, you haven't seen the half of it yet. Atlanta's like a puzzle – the more pieces you discover, the crazier it gets."

Zy interjected with a ghetto-infused excitement, "Charmz here is the maestro of the dance floor, honey! Ain't nobody move like him in the A."

Malik blushed modestly, "Aw, Zy exaggerating, as always. But seriously, Tachelle, you gotta embrace the rhythm of this city. It's like a heartbeat – once it gets into your veins, you can't resist."

Tachelle nodded, captivated by Malik's charisma. "I'll keep that in mind. Any tips for surviving the Atlanta dance?"

Malik grinned, "Rule number one: Let the music speak to your soul. Everything else will fall into place."

Their conversation unfolded seamlessly, Malik sharing stories of his journey into the Atlanta dance scene, the highs, and lows of chasing dreams in the city's heartbeat. As the night wore on, Tachelle found herself drawn not only to the pulsating rhythms of the Starlight Lounge but to the vibrant personalities that painted the city's canvas.

Little did she know that this encounter with Malik would be a stepping stone into a realm where the echoes of Atlanta's dreams would intertwine with the untold stories of those who danced beneath the city lights.

As the night unfolded at the Starlight Lounge, the trio's laughter and shared stories echoed through the dimly lit space. The rhythmic beats seemed to synchronize with the lively conversations, creating a backdrop that blended seamlessly with the vibrant energy of the city.

Malik's denim jacket, adorned with patches that told stories of his journey through Atlanta's eclectic subcultures, added an extra layer of charm to his already magnetic presence. His lean, athletic frame moved with grace, a testament to the countless hours spent perfecting his craft.

"So, Tachelle, what brought you to Atlanta? Must be more than just the dreams of business school," Malik inquired, a mischievous glint in his eyes.

Tachelle, sipping on a fruity cocktail, opened up about her aspirations and the challenges she faced since arriving in the city. "I came here to study business at Clark Atlanta, but reality hit me hard. Everything's so different from Jackson, and, well, money doesn't grow on trees."

Malik nodded in understanding. "Atlanta's a beast, no doubt. But it's also a city that rewards resilience. You gotta hustle, but the rewards are worth it."

Zy, interjecting with her rachet and ghetto-infused enthusiasm, added, "That's right, Charmz! Tachelle, let me tell you, this city got secrets, and we're just scratching the surface. You need to embrace it all – the hustle, the heartbreaks, and the victories."

Tachelle, intrigued by the mysterious allure of Atlanta, leaned in. "Secrets? What do you mean?"

Zy, with a sly smile, glanced around before leaning closer. "Honey, Atlanta's more than just concrete and skyscrapers. There's a whole underground scene, and you gotta have the right connections to uncover it."

Malik, sharing a knowing look with Zy, chimed in, "Zy's talking about the real heartbeat of Atlanta – the hidden spots, the exclusive events. It's like a secret society, and once you're in, your Atlanta experience transforms."

Tachelle, her curiosity piqued, couldn't help but be drawn into the enigma that surrounded the city. The night continued, a tapestry of shared dreams, secret whispers, and the beats that united them all.

As the trio exited the Starlight Lounge into the cool Atlanta night, the city's secrets seemed to linger in the air. Tachelle, now part of this newfound alliance, was on the cusp of a journey that transcended textbooks and business plans. Little did she know, the echoes of Atlanta's dreams were about to crescendo into a symphony of experiences, with Malik and Zy as her guides through the city's clandestine corridors.

"Where to next?" Tachelle asked, her eyes sparkling with anticipation.

Zy smiled mischievously. "There's a spot just a few blocks from here. It's an underground club that doesn't even have a name. Only the locals know about it."

Malik nodded, his grin wide. "Trust us, Tachelle. Tonight, you're about to see a side of Atlanta most people never experience."

As they walked through the labyrinthine streets, Tachelle felt a mix of excitement and trepidation. The city, with its endless possibilities and hidden depths, was starting to reveal itself to her in ways she had never imagined. The night air was cool against her skin, and the distant sounds of the city created a symphony that resonated within her.

They arrived at an unmarked door in an alleyway, the entrance guarded by a burly man with a stern expression. Malik exchanged a few words with him, and the door swung open, revealing a staircase that led down into the pulsating heart of Atlanta's underground.

The club was a sensory overload. Neon lights cast a surreal glow over the crowd, and the music was a hypnotic blend of electronic beats and soulful melodies. Tachelle felt herself being drawn into the rhythm, her body moving almost instinctively to the music.

"Welcome to the real Atlanta," Zy shouted over the music, her eyes shining with excitement.

Malik led them to a corner where a group of dancers were performing an impromptu routine. Their movements were fluid and expressive, telling stories through their dance. Tachelle watched in awe, feeling a deep connection to the raw emotion and energy that filled the room.

"This is incredible," she said, her voice barely audible over the music.

Malik nodded. "This is where the magic happens. This is where you find the true spirit of Atlanta."

As the night wore on, Tachelle lost herself in the music and the vibrant energy of the club. She danced with Zy and Malik, their movements a testament to the unspoken bond that was forming between them. In that moment, she felt a sense of belonging she had never experienced before.

When they finally emerged from the club in the early hours of the morning, the city was bathed in the soft light of dawn. Tachelle felt a sense of exhilaration and exhaustion, her mind racing with the events of the night.

"Thank you," she said, her voice filled with gratitude. "I don't think I'll ever forget this night."

Zy smiled, her eyes twinkling. "This is just the beginning, Tachelle. Welcome to Atlanta."

As they made their way back to their apartments, Tachelle couldn't help but feel that her life was about to change in ways she had never imagined. The pain behind the pole, the struggle to find her place in the world, was still there, but now it was accompanied by the promise of new beginnings and the hope of a brighter future. With Zy and Malik by her side, she felt ready to face whatever challenges lay ahead, knowing that the echoes of Atlanta's dreams would guide her on her journey.

Chapter 3: Beneath the Surface

The sun was barely up when Tachelle's phone buzzed, interrupting the peaceful silence of her apartment. It was Zy, her voice as vibrant as ever despite the late night.

"Morning, sunshine! You ready to dive into another day in the A?" Zy asked, her enthusiasm contagious.

Tachelle rubbed her eyes and smiled. "Barely awake, but yeah, I'm ready."

"Good! Get dressed and meet me at the café on Auburn Avenue. I've got something exciting to show you," Zy said before hanging up.

Tachelle dressed quickly, choosing a simple but stylish outfit: a fitted black top, high-waisted jeans, and her favorite sneakers. She took a moment to glance at herself in the mirror, feeling a surge of determination. Atlanta was proving to be everything she hoped for and more.

When she arrived at the café, Zy was already there, sipping a cappuccino and chatting animatedly with a barista. She waved Tachelle over and handed her a latte.

"Got you your favorite," Zy said with a wink.

"Thanks, Zy. What's this exciting thing you mentioned?" Tachelle asked, taking a grateful sip of her drink.

"Remember Malik's talk about the hidden side of Atlanta? We're going to dig a bit deeper today. There's an art gallery downtown that hosts some of the most avant-garde exhibitions. It's invite-only, but Charmz managed to get us in," Zy explained, her eyes gleaming with excitement.

Tachelle felt a thrill run through her. The night at the Starlight Lounge had opened her eyes to the city's vibrant undercurrent, and she was eager to explore more.

They finished their coffees and headed to the gallery. The building was unassuming from the outside, but as soon as they stepped in, Tachelle was struck by the explosion of colors and textures that adorned the walls. The gallery was alive with creativity, each piece telling a unique story.

Malik greeted them at the entrance, his denim jacket replaced by a sleek, black blazer. "Glad you could make it, Tachelle. Welcome to the Art Haven."

As they walked through the exhibits, Malik introduced them to various artists, each with a distinct style and perspective. Tachelle was particularly drawn to a series of paintings that depicted scenes from everyday life in Atlanta, rendered in vibrant hues that captured the city's energy.

One artist, a young woman with a shaved head and intricate tattoos, approached them. "Hey, I'm Candice. Glad you like my work," she said, nodding toward the paintings.

"These are incredible," Tachelle said, her eyes still fixed on the artwork. "They really capture the spirit of the city."

"Thanks. Atlanta's got a lot of stories to tell, and I try to bring them to life through my art," Kendra replied, her voice tinged with passion.

As they continued to explore, Tachelle found herself immersed in conversations with the artists, each encounter adding another layer to her understanding of the city. She felt a growing connection to Atlanta, as if the city's heartbeat was syncing with her own.

After a few hours, they left the gallery, the afternoon sun casting long shadows on the streets. Tachelle felt invigorated, her mind buzzing with inspiration.

"That was amazing, Malik. Thank you for inviting us," Tachelle said as they walked back to their cars.

"Anytime. There's so much more to discover, Tachelle. Atlanta's got layers, and each one is more fascinating than the last," Malik replied, his smile warm and genuine.

Zy linked arms with Tachelle. "And we're just getting started, girl. Tonight, there's a spoken word event at a little spot called 'Whispers'. You in?"

Tachelle nodded eagerly. "Absolutely."

The rest of the day flew by, and before she knew it, Tachelle was getting ready for the evening. She chose a flowy dress that made her feel confident and comfortable, her short dreadlocks styled neatly.

"Whispers" was a cozy, dimly lit venue tucked away in a quiet neighborhood. The atmosphere was intimate, with candles on the tables and soft music playing in the background. Zy and Malik were already there, sitting with a group of people who welcomed Tachelle warmly.

The spoken word event began, and Tachelle was mesmerized by the performers. Each poet poured their heart out, their words weaving intricate tapestries of emotion and experience. Tachelle felt a deep connection to their stories, their struggles, and their triumphs.

One poet, a tall man with dreadlocks and a deep, resonant voice, took the stage and began to speak. His poem was a powerful reflection on identity and resilience, touching on themes that resonated deeply with Tachelle.

As the night went on, Tachelle felt a sense of belonging she hadn't expected to find so quickly. The people she met, the stories she heard, and the experiences she shared all contributed to a growing sense of home.

After the event, they lingered outside, the warm night air filled with the sounds of laughter and conversation.

"Tonight was incredible," Tachelle said, her voice filled with emotion. "Thank you both for bringing me here."

"You're one of us now, Tachelle. Welcome to the family," Zy said, giving her a tight hug.

Malik nodded. "This city has a way of bringing people together. I'm glad you're here to experience it with us."

As Tachelle walked back to her apartment, she felt a deep sense of contentment. The pain behind the pole, the struggles she had faced, were still a part of her, but they were now accompanied by the promise of new beginnings and the support of newfound friends. Atlanta was becoming her city, and she was ready to embrace all it had to offer.

Chapter 4: Dancing on the Edge

The next morning, Tachelle found herself sitting on her small balcony, sipping a cup of tea and watching the city wake up. Her mind kept drifting back to the previous night, replaying the conversations and the sense of community she felt at "Whispers". She had never felt so alive, so in tune with her surroundings.

Her phone buzzed, breaking her reverie. It was a message from Zy: "Brunch at my place? Got something to discuss."

Intrigued, Tachelle quickly got ready and made her way to Zy's apartment, a chic loft in a trendy part of town. The moment she stepped inside, she was enveloped by the comforting aroma of freshly brewed coffee and the sight of a beautifully set brunch table.

"Hey, girl!" Zy greeted her with a hug. "Help yourself to whatever you like."

Tachelle filled her plate with fresh fruit, pastries, and scrambled eggs, and they sat down by the window, which offered a stunning view of the city.

"So, Tachelle," Zy began, her tone a mix of curiosity and concern, "how are things going for you? Really going?"

Tachelle sighed, setting her fork down. "Honestly, it's been tough. The move here, the cost of living, school expenses... it's all starting to pile up. I'm trying to make ends meet, but it's harder than I thought."

Zy nodded, her eyes sympathetic. "I figured as much. That's why I wanted to talk to you today."

Tachelle looked at her, curiosity piqued. "What do you mean?"

Zy took a deep breath, as if carefully choosing her words. "I know we haven't talked much about what I do for a living. The truth is, I'm an exotic dancer. I work at a club called 'Velvet Dreams.'"

Tachelle blinked, surprised but not judgmental. "Really? I had no idea."

Zy nodded. "Yeah, it's not something I broadcast, but it pays the bills and then some. It's how I afford to live comfortably here. And... I wanted to suggest it as an option for you."

Tachelle's eyes widened. "Me? Dancing? I don't know, Zy. I've never even considered something like that."

Zy reached across the table and took Tachelle's hand. "I get it, Tachelle. It's not for everyone. But you're beautiful, confident, and you have this natural charm that would do well on stage. Plus, the money is good. Really good."

Tachelle's mind raced with thoughts and emotions. She had never imagined herself in such a role, but the financial struggles she was facing were real and pressing.

"I don't know, Zy. It sounds... intimidating," Tachelle admitted.

Zy squeezed her hand. "I understand. It's not something you have to decide right away. But if you want, I can take you to the club, let you see what it's like. No pressure, just an opportunity to explore."

Tachelle nodded slowly. "Okay. I'll go with you, just to see."

Zy smiled warmly. "That's all I ask. And remember, no matter what you decide, I'm here for you."

Later that evening, Zy and Tachelle headed to "Velvet Dreams". The exterior of the club was sleek and modern, with neon lights casting a soft glow on the entrance. Zy led Tachelle inside, where they were greeted by a friendly bouncer who nodded in recognition.

The interior was dimly lit, with plush seating and a stage that dominated the room. The atmosphere was surprisingly inviting, with soft music playing and an air of sophistication. Zy guided Tachelle to a table near the stage.

As they sat down, a waitress brought over drinks. Zy took a sip of her cocktail and leaned in. "This is where I work, Tachelle. It's not what most people think. It's about performance, about feeling empowered."

Tachelle watched as a dancer took the stage, her movements fluid and mesmerizing. The crowd watched in awe, and Tachelle found herself captivated by the dancer's grace and confidence. The performance was an art form, each movement telling a story and exuding strength.

"Wow," Tachelle whispered, unable to take her eyes off the stage. "She's incredible."

Zy smiled. "Her name's Lila. She's been dancing here for years. It's not just about the money for her; it's about the freedom and the expression."

As the performance continued, Tachelle's initial apprehension began to fade, replaced by a sense of curiosity and intrigue. She could see the allure of the stage, the way it offered a form of liberation and a way to reclaim one's own narrative.

After Lila's performance, Zy introduced Tachelle to some of the other dancers. They were a diverse group, each with their own unique style and story. They welcomed Tachelle warmly, sharing their experiences and insights.

One dancer, a petite woman with vibrant purple hair, approached Tachelle with a friendly smile. "Hey there, I'm Jade. Zy told us a bit about you. Thinking about joining our little family?"

Tachelle smiled shyly. "I'm just exploring the idea. It's all so new to me."

Jade nodded. "I get it. When I first started, I was terrified. But once I got on that stage, I found a part of myself I didn't know existed. It's empowering."

Another dancer, a tall woman with an athletic build, chimed in. "And the money is a huge plus. I paid off my student loans and bought a car within my first year. It's hard work, but it's rewarding."

Tachelle listened intently, absorbing their words. She felt a connection to these women, their stories resonating with her own journey of self-discovery and resilience.

As the night went on, Zy showed Tachelle around the club, introducing her to the staff and explaining how everything worked. She emphasized the importance of boundaries and the support system among the dancers.

"We look out for each other here," Zy said. "It's like a sisterhood. If you decide to give it a try, you'll have all of us backing you up."

By the time they left the club, Tachelle's mind was swirling with thoughts and possibilities. She had come to Atlanta with dreams of success, and now she was faced with a new path that could offer both financial stability and a chance to discover a different side of herself.

They walked back to Zy's car in comfortable silence, the night air cool and refreshing. As they reached the car, Tachelle turned to Zy, her eyes reflecting a mix of determination and uncertainty.

"Zy, thank you for showing me this. I never would have considered it if it weren't for you."

Zy smiled warmly. "You're welcome, Tachelle. Just remember, whatever you decide, I'm here for you. You have the strength to do anything you set your mind to."

Tachelle nodded, feeling a newfound sense of empowerment. "I'll think about it. Really think about it."

Over the next few days, Tachelle couldn't shake the thoughts of "Velvet Dreams" and the possibilities it presented. She weighed the pros and cons, considering the financial relief it could bring and the personal growth it might foster.

Finally, one evening, as she sat in her apartment reflecting on her journey so far, she made a decision. She picked up her phone and called Zy.

"Hey, Zy. I've been thinking a lot, and... I want to give it a try. I want to dance."

Zy's voice was filled with pride and excitement. "That's great, Tachelle! I knew you had it in you. We'll start slow, and I'll be with you every step of the way."

Tachelle felt a mixture of nerves and exhilaration. She was stepping into uncharted territory, but she was ready. Ready to embrace the challenges and opportunities that lay ahead, and ready to discover the strength and resilience within herself.

The next chapter of her Atlanta journey was about to begin, and Tachelle was determined to make it her own.

THE FOLLOWING WEEK, Tachelle found herself back at "Velvet Dreams," this time not as a curious visitor but as an aspiring dancer. Zy had arranged for her to meet with the club's manager, a tall, elegant woman named Simone.

"Welcome, Tachelle," Simone greeted her with a warm smile. "Zy speaks very highly of you. Are you ready to take the first step?"

Tachelle nodded, her heart pounding. "I am. I'm ready."

Simone led her through the process, explaining the rules, the schedule, and the expectations. She emphasized the importance of confidence and self-assurance, qualities Tachelle was eager to cultivate.

Zy was by her side the entire time, offering encouragement and support. "You've got this, Tachelle. Just be yourself and let your natural charm shine through."

Tachelle took a deep breath, feeling a mix of nerves and excitement. She changed into a simple yet elegant outfit, a black bodysuit that accentuated her curves while allowing her to move freely. As she stood backstage, waiting for her turn, she felt a surge of determination.

When her name was called, Tachelle stepped onto the stage, the spotlight illuminating her. The music began, a slow, sultry rhythm that matched the beating of her heart. She took a deep breath and started to move, letting the music guide her.

At first, her movements were tentative, but as she found her rhythm, she began to relax. She remembered Zy's words about empowerment and expression, and she let herself go, dancing with a confidence she didn't know she possessed.

The audience watched in rapt attention, captivated by Tachelle's performance. She felt their energy, their support, and it fueled her movements. For the first time, she felt truly free, unburdened by doubts or insecurities.

When the music ended, the room erupted in applause. Tachelle stood there, breathless and exhilarated, a smile spreading across her face. She had done it. She had taken the first step.

Backstage, Zy enveloped her in a tight hug. "I knew you could do it! You were amazing, Tachelle!"

Tachelle beamed, her heart swelling with pride. "Thank you, Zy. For everything."

Simone approached, her eyes filled with approval. "Well done, Tachelle. Welcome to 'Velvet Dreams'. I think you're going to fit in just fine."

As Tachelle left the club that night, she felt a sense of accomplishment and hope. She was ready to embrace this new chapter, to explore the depths of her potential and to rise above the challenges that lay ahead.

Atlanta was her city now, and she was determined to dance through its highs and lows, to uncover the hidden stories and to create her own. The pain behind the pole was still there, but so was the promise of new beginnings, of strength, and of a future she was ready to claim.

The next night which was her first official night on the job went well.

The DJ's voice boomed over the loudspeaker, adding an element of glamour to the atmosphere. "Ladies and gentlemen, get ready for a sizzling show! Please welcome to the stage our newest sensation... Mahogany!"

The name echoed through the club, marking the birth of Tachelle's stripper identity. From this point forward, she would be known by different names – Tachelle, Chelle, Mahogany, or simply Mah – each representing a facet of her journey in the mesmerizing world of Velvet Dreams.

As the DJ's announcement faded, Tachelle, now Mahogany, stepped onto the stage. The spotlight embraced her as the opening notes of "Bad Bad" by Hunxho filled the air. The music, a pulsating beat that matched the rhythm of the city itself, guided Mahogany's movements.

Her performance was a dance of liberation, a display of sensuality intertwined with empowerment. The audience was captivated by Mahogany's magnetic presence, her movements synchronized with the melody. The luminescent lights cast a spell, creating an ethereal glow around her as she twirled and spun, a testament to her newfound confidence.

As the song reached its climax, Mahogany descended from the pole, the applause of the audience filling the club. The journey of Tachelle into the persona of Mahogany had begun, a luminescent chapter in the vibrant tapestry of Atlanta's nightlife.

The applause lingered in the air as Mahogany gracefully exited the stage, the vibrant energy of Velvet Dreams enveloping her. Zy, waiting backstage, greeted her with a triumphant smile.

"Girl, you killed it out there! Mahogany is a name they won't forget," Zy exclaimed, a camaraderie forming between them.

As Mahogany navigated the bustling atmosphere of the club, patrons and fellow dancers acknowledged her newfound presence. Some called her Tachelle, others Chelle, and a few referred to her simply as Mah. The multiplicity of identities embraced her, each name holding a unique resonance in the varied narratives unfolding within Velvet Dreams.

Lorenzo Wilkins, known as Renz, observed from the shadows, captivated by Mahogany's performance. The luminescent dance had cast a spell, weaving connections that would shape the destiny of those entangled in the vibrant tapestry of Atlanta's nightlife.

Outside the club's neon embrace, the city pulsated with life. Mahogany, with each step, was becoming a symbol – a luminescent presence in the dimly lit corners of Atlanta's secrets. The night held promises and shadows, and Mahogany was poised to navigate the dichotomy, guided by the rhythm of the city and the secrets that whispered in its streets.

The night at Velvet Dreams unfolded like a symphony of desires, each dancer a note contributing to the intoxicating melody. Mahogany, having left an indelible mark with her debut, found herself navigating the intricate social dynamics of the strip club.

As she moved through the dimly lit corridors, a fellow dancer named Crystal approached with a mix of curiosity and camaraderie. "Hey, Mah! That was one hell of a performance. You got some moves. Welcome to the family!"

Mahogany, appreciating the warmth, smiled. "Thanks, Crystal. I'm still finding my way around here."

Crystal, with a mischievous glint in her eye, leaned in. "Girl, you're gonna learn fast. Just remember, it's not just about the dance; it's about the game. Keep your eyes open and your heels high."

The advice lingered as Mahogany continued her journey through Velvet Dreams The dimly lit VIP lounge beckoned, where patrons sought a more intimate connection with the dancers. Mahogany, navigating this new terrain, encountered a regular named Marcus – a middle-aged businessman with a penchant for the allure of the night.

"Mahogany, my favorite new addition. Care to join me for a drink?" Marcus inquired, a glimmer of familiarity in his eyes.

Mahogany, embracing the role, took a seat, engaging in a delicate dance of conversation and charm. As the night progressed, she found herself entangled in the intricate web of relationships that defined the dynamic world of Velvet Dreams.

The luminescence of the club cast shadows on secrets, desires, and the pursuit of dreams. Mahogany, now a player in this nocturnal symphony, moved through the night with a blend of grace and allure, navigating the complexities of Atlanta's clandestine corridors.

As the closing hours approached, Mahogany stepped into the cool Atlanta night, the echoes of the club's rhythm still resonating within her. The city held its secrets, and Mahogany, with each step, embraced the duality of the life she had chosen – a dance between shadows and luminescence in the heart of Atlanta's nightlife.

Back at her apartment, Tachelle, still buzzing from the night's events, collapsed onto her couch. She stared at the ceiling, her mind replaying the evening's performance. The excitement, the applause, the rush of adrenaline—it was all intoxicating. Yet, she couldn't shake the feeling of stepping into a world far removed from the one she had known.

The following afternoon, Zy came over with takeout and a bottle of wine to celebrate. They settled on the couch, the familiar scent of Chinese food filling the air.

"How are you feeling after last night?" Zy asked, pouring them each a glass of wine.

Tachelle took a sip, savoring the sweet relief. "I feel... amazing. Nervous, but amazing. I never thought I could do something like that."

Zy grinned. "You were incredible, Mah. You have this natural grace and power on stage. It's like you were born for it."

Tachelle blushed. "Thanks, Zy. I couldn't have done it without you."

They clinked glasses, a silent toast to new beginnings. As they ate, Zy shared more about the ins and outs of the club, offering tips and advice.

"One thing you have to remember," Zy said, her tone turning serious, "is to keep your head in the game. It's easy to get lost in the nightlife, but you need to stay focused on your goals."

Tachelle nodded, absorbing her words. "I will. I have to."

Chapter 5: The Charismatic Arrival of Renz

The night unfolded in the dimly lit corners of Atlanta as the charismatic Lorenzo Wilkins, known as Renz, made his entrance into the pulsating heart of Velvet Dreams. Renz carried with him a mysterious aura, shaped by the shadows of his past.

Born and bred in the mean streets of Atlanta's Westside, Renz was no stranger to the hustle and grind. His journey, carved by the unforgiving concrete, molded him into a natural-born finesser. As tales of street life whispered through the air, Renz emerged as a figure of resilience and strategic brilliance.

Standing at 6'1, Renz commanded attention with a cool calm demeanor that masked the complexities beneath the surface. His hair, cut in a low fade, created an ocean-like wave pattern cascading across the crown of his head. Watchful eyes, sharp and calculating, absorbed the nuances of the environment around him.

On this particular night, Renz donned an ensemble that echoed both style and opulence. Baby blue stacked Valabasas jeans adorned his frame, cinched by a bejeweled B.B. Simmons belt that whispered tales of a lavish lifestyle. A white and blue Vlone t-shirt, accompanied by a Currency Apparel ski mask rolled atop his head like a makeshift beanie. Wrist adorned with a bust-down diamond Cartier Skeleton watch, Renz's timepiece was in fierce competition with the chunked-up Cuban link chain that graced his neck. Every element of his attire was a statement, a visual symphony of wealth and street charisma.

As Renz moved through the neon-lit corridors of Velvet Dreams, his charismatic presence shifted the atmosphere. Patrons turned their heads, and dancers paused mid-motion to catch a glimpse of the man whose reputation echoed through the city.

Approaching the bar where Zy awaited, Renz's eyes scanned the room until they settled on the rising star, Mahogany, preparing for her performance on the stage. The luminescent glow of the club seemed to intensify as Renz's watchful eyes followed her every move.

Zy, sipping her drink, acknowledged Renz's arrival with a subtle nod. "Renz, you always know how to make an entrance."

Renz, a master of understated charm, responded with a smirk. "It's an art, Zy. Now, where's our rising star, Mahogany?"

Zy gestured towards the stage, where Mahogany, unaware of Renz's presence, prepared for her upcoming performance. The luminescent glow of the club seemed to intensify as Renz's watchful eyes followed her every move. As Mahogany took the spotlight, Renz leaned against the bar, his cool calm demeanor unwavering. The echoes of the city's rhythm intertwined with the pulsating beats of the club, creating an ambiance that suited Renz's enigmatic presence.

The charismatic arrival of Renz marked the beginning of a chapter that promised intrigue and allure. His watchful eyes followed Mahogany's dance, a performance that resonated with a magnetic energy. Renz, a figure shaped by the shadows of the Westside, observed with a mix of pride and contemplation.

As Mahogany descended from the stage, the room filled with applause. Renz, his ocean-like waves of hair catching the neon glow, approached Zy with a glint of anticipation. "Zy, my dear, looks like we've got something special in Mahogany."

Zy, her eyes reflecting a shared history with Renz, nodded knowingly. "Keep watching, Renz. Atlanta's nights are full of surprises."

As Renz and Zy engaged in casual banter at the bar, the echoes of their shared past lingered beneath the surface. There was a time when they were more than just acquaintances, a moment in their lives when passion flared between them like a wild flame.

In the shadowy recesses of Atlanta's Westside, Renz and Zy had shared more than just glances. Their past, marked by an intense sexual chemistry, had blossomed into a brief liaison. However, both astute in their understanding of the impracticality of a long-term commitment, decided to part ways amicably.

Their connection didn't dissolve entirely; instead, it transformed into a unique camaraderie. Zy, always resourceful, occasionally played matchmaker, bringing girls into Renz's life for various purposes, including music video appearances for his rap artist friends.

Meanwhile, on the other side of the club, Mahogany finished her performance, the seductive rhythm still lingering in the air. Renz, having observed her dance with an intrigued gaze, decided it was time for their paths to cross.

With a magnetic presence, Renz approached Mahogany, his ocean-like waves of hair catching the neon glow. "Well, well, Mahogany. That was quite a performance. I couldn't help but be captivated."

Mahogany, slightly shy yet emboldened by her newfound role, met Renz's gaze. "Thank you. It's my job to captivate, after all."

Renz, displaying his dominant, suggestive charm, leaned in slightly. "You do more than just captivate. You entrance. What's your story, Mahogany?"

Mahogany, a mix of awe and courage, replied, "Just a small-town girl trying to make it in the big city."

Their conversation unfolded like a dance, a flirtatious exchange with an undercurrent of desire. However, the magnetic pull between Renz and Mahogany didn't go unnoticed. Charmz, watching from a distance, felt a twinge of jealousy and envy. Unbeknownst to Mahogany, Charmz harbored a hidden desire for her, and witnessing the flirtatious interaction with Renz fueled his frustration. As the night progressed, the dynamics within Velvet Dreams continued to evolve, weaving a complex tapestry of desires, past connections, and the magnetic allure of Atlanta's nightlife.

As the night unfolded, Renz and Mahogany found themselves caught in the rhythmic dance of Atlanta's nightlife. Their interactions grew more frequent, each encounter deepening the connection that seemed to transcend the dimly lit corridors of Velvet Dreams.

Renz, recognizing the allure of Mahogany's presence, took deliberate steps to navigate the uncharted territories of their budding relationship. He showered her with attention, leaving no doubt about his interest. Flowers arrived at her doorstep, and surprises appeared in unexpected moments – tokens of affection that spoke louder than words.

Mahogany, initially shy, found herself drawn to Renz's charisma and the genuine efforts he made to showcase his feelings. Their conversations evolved into shared laughter, whispered secrets, and a growing sense of intimacy that mirrored the shadows cast by the neon glow.

One evening, Renz orchestrated a surprise – a rooftop dinner overlooking the city. The table adorned with candles, the skyline providing a breathtaking backdrop, set the stage for a moment of shared vulnerability. Over the course of the evening, Renz and Mahogany delved into their pasts, dreams, and desires, each revelation forging a deeper bond.

As Renz continued to pursue Mahogany's heart, his actions spoke of a man willing to go to extra lengths to prove his love and loyalty. He attended her performances with unwavering support, his applause echoing louder than the rest. Renz became a constant presence, not just in the neon-lit haven of Velvet Dreams but in the fabric of Mahogany's life. In a gesture that resonated beyond the walls of the strip club, Renz surprised Mahogany with a visit to Clark Atlanta University, where she once dreamt of studying business. The symbolic act spoke of an understanding that transcended the glitz and glamour of their nocturnal world.

Mahogany, touched by Renz's efforts, found herself grappling with emotions that extended beyond the allure of the stage. Their connection, though born in the neon-lit embrace of Velvet Dreams, grew roots that reached into the depths of their hearts.

As the nights turned into days, Renz's charisma and Mahogany's allure became entwined in a love story that defied the conventions of their respective worlds. The city's rhythm played witness to their unfolding tale, a symphony of desires and shadows that echoed through the heart of Atlanta.

Three months had slipped away since the first spark between Renz and Mahogany ignited, evolving into a profound infatuation. The once lingering shadows of uncertainty had transformed into a certainty that spoke of intertwined hearts, minds, and souls.

Within the neon-lit embrace of "Exquisite's," Renz found himself yearning for something more profound than the nocturnal world they inhabited. The realization struck him—his feelings for Mahogany had matured into something deep and meaningful. Their love story unfolded discreetly in the dimly lit corners of the club.

In a pivotal moment, Renz approached Grant Styles, the manager of "Exquisite's," with a proposal to grant Mahogany a weekend off. The calm, collected exterior that defined Renz cracked as Grant, in a slightly tipsy state, dismissed the request without consideration. Suppressing the fiery anger simmering beneath, Renz sought common ground.

"I just want a couple of days for Mahogany. I'm willing to compensate you for the inconvenience."

Grant, unfazed, rejected the proposal with disdain. Attempting to maintain composure, Renz pulled out a stack of money.

"Just let me know how much, and it's no pressure."

Grant's dismissive response triggered a dormant volcano within Renz. In a swift motion, he grabbed Grant by the throat, fury boiling over.

As Grant gasped for air, Renz delivered a chilling ultimatum.

"You're going to give Mahogany those days off, a bonus, and start renegotiating her fee. You understand?"

Terrified, Grant nodded in agreement.

Once the confrontation ended, Renz smoothed out his shirt, wiped the sweat from his face, and casually pocketed a box of Cuban cigars. The club, silent witnesses to the unexpected turn of events, stared wide-eyed as Renz made his exit.

With the weekend secured, Renz arranged a surprise getaway to Las Vegas, chartering a private jet for a luxurious escape. The city lights mirrored the dazzling glow of the diamond ring and the chain with his name in bold baguettes that Renz gifted Mahogany. As the jet soared into the night sky, Renz handed her a key to his condo, symbolizing a commitment that extended beyond the boundaries of "Exquisite's." He asked her to move in with him, urging her to pack up her things as soon as they returned.

IN LAS VEGAS, THE COUPLE indulged in the opulence of the Bellagio Hotel, where luxury surrounded them at every turn. Renz, determined to show Mahogany a world she had never experienced, led her to renowned casinos and exquisite restaurants, each moment adding to the tapestry of their budding romance.

As they strolled the vibrant streets of Las Vegas, the city's heartbeat resonated with the rhythm of their love. In an intimate moment, Renz presented Mahogany with the chain displaying his name, the dazzling diamond ring, and a key that held a profound promise.

"This is not just the key to my spot but the key to my heart. You are the first to ever receive either, Mah. I believe in you; don't let me down," Renz whispered.

Overwhelmed by the grandeur of her surroundings and the depth of Renz's love, Mahogany felt a surge of emotions. Being on a private jet for the first time, pampered and cherished by a man in ways she had never imagined, Mahogany's heart swelled with gratitude. The gift of the key symbolized not just access to a physical space but entry into the sanctuary of Renz's heart.

As they embraced in the glow of the Las Vegas lights, their love story reached new heights, transcending the boundaries of their nocturnal world. Each moment spent together solidified their bond, weaving together dreams and aspirations that danced beneath the surface of their lavish escapades. The city of sin became a backdrop for their burgeoning love, a testament to the depths of their connection beyond the pulsing lights and glamour.

Chapter 6: Whispers of Desire

Las Vegas's glittering lights had faded into the distance as Renz and Mahogany returned from their whirlwind escape. The private jet touched down softly on the tarmac of Atlanta, marking the beginning of a new chapter in their love story. Mahogany's heart raced with a mix of excitement and uncertainty as she stepped off the plane, feeling Renz's reassuring presence beside her.

"You're mine, Mah. This is just the beginning," Renz murmured, his voice a velvety promise that lingered in the cool night air. Mahogany smiled, her hand entwined with his, the weight of the chain around her neck and the sparkle of the diamond ring reminding her of their unspoken vows.

Their return to Velvet Dreams was met with a subtle shift in dynamics. The club buzzed with its usual energy, neon lights casting a hypnotic glow on the nocturnal haven. Renz and Mahogany, however, seemed to exist in a world apart, their connection palpable amidst the swirling smoke and pulsating beats.

One night, as the neon lights flickered in rhythmic patterns, Charmz found Mahogany in the dimly lit corridors of Velvet Dreams. Concern etched lines of worry on his face as he approached her.

"Mah, you've been changing since Renz came into the picture. I've heard things, rumors about him, his business dealings. I just want you to be careful," Charmz whispered, his tone filled with genuine concern.

Mahogany turned to face him, her eyes reflecting a fierce loyalty. "Charmz, you need to stop listening to gossip. Renz is not involved in any shady business. He's a good man, and I won't let anyone tarnish his name," she declared, her voice resonating through the corridor.

Caught off guard by Mahogany's fierce defense, Charmz stammered to respond. The club's pulsating beats seemed to pause momentarily as the two engaged in a verbal dance of conflicting perspectives.

"Mah, I'm just looking out for you. There's talk about Renz's past, the things he's done. You need to be careful," Charmz persisted, trying to express his concern.

Mahogany remained unwavering, dismissing the rumors with a shake of her head. "Renz has changed. He's not the person he used to be. Don't believe everything you hear," she retorted, her words cutting through the air.

As the weeks unfolded, Renz's presence at Velvet Dreams became more pronounced. His aura, a magnetic force that drew attention, whispered of desire and power. The atmosphere shifted as Renz navigated the space with effortless charm, his eyes always finding Mahogany in the crowd, reassuring her with a glance.

Charmz, watching from a distance, observed the transformation in Mahogany. The envy in her eyes reflected the silent acknowledgment of Renz's hidden desires. A subtle tension lingered, adding a layer of complexity to the dynamics within Velvet Dreams.

Behind the scenes, Renz orchestrated plans to secure Mahogany's future, subtly influencing the club's management without their awareness of his deeper intentions. The positive changes in the club's atmosphere were welcomed, masking the clandestine moves being made.

As Renz and Mahogany danced between the shadows of desire and the bright lights of the club, their love story unfolded like a clandestine symphony. Every glance, every touch, spoke volumes of a passion that refused to be confined within the walls of Velvet Dreams.

One evening, Renz set in motion a surprise for Mahogany, orchestrating an event that would showcase her talents and affirm her place in his heart. The club's neon lights dimmed in anticipation as Mahogany stepped onto the stage, a spotlight enveloping her in a halo of light. The audience hushed in reverence.

"Ladies and gentlemen, give it up for the one and only, Mahogany!"

The beat of the music filled the air as Mahogany unleashed a mesmerizing pole performance. Her movements were fluid, a testament to the hours spent perfecting each routine. The crowd erupted in cheers, captivated by the raw sensuality and grace of her dance.

Renz, positioned at the edge of the stage, watched with an intensity that bordered on possessiveness. Mahogany's eyes met his, and in that moment, the connection between them transcended the boundaries of the club, a silent vow exchanged amid the applause and adoration.

The performance reached its climax, and Mahogany descended from the pole, her body glistening with sweat and adulation. Renz approached her with a mix of pride and desire evident in his eyes.

"You killed it, Mah. You always do," Renz whispered, his words a caress against her ear.

Mahogany, breathless but beaming, responded, "All for you, Renz."

As they shared a private moment amid the neon glow, the whispers of desire continued to weave their way through the fabric of Velvet Dreams. The night held promises of passion and the subtle interplay of love and lust, a tapestry woven with their shared desires and aspirations.

In the dimly lit corridors, Charmz observed the scene, his earlier concerns still lingering. The whispers of Renz's mysterious past and the rumors surrounding the club's enigmatic owner cast a shadow over the dazzling performance, creating a subtle tension in the air that refused to dissipate.

The night pressed on, a canvas painted with desire, passion, and the unknown. As the neon lights continued their rhythmic dance, Mahogany and Renz disappeared into the shadows of Velvet Dreams, their love story unfolding in the whispers of the night, destined to leave an indelible mark on the fabric of their lives.

Chapter 7: Shadows of Love and Deceit

Mahogany's life with Renz unfolded in a whirlwind of luxury and desire, but shadows began to creep into the corners of her fairy-tale romance. The neon glow of Velvet Dreams couldn't shield her from the darker aspects of Renz's world.

Tachelle, now fully immersed in her new identity as Mahogany, reveled in the opulence that Renz provided. The lavish penthouse, adorned with decadence, served as a backdrop to their escalating relationship. Yet, subtle moments of tension seeped in like cracks forming in the facade of their perfect love story.

One evening, as they shared a quiet moment in their expansive living room, a sudden change in Renz's demeanor caught Mahogany off guard. The soft whispers of love were replaced by an unsettling silence, shadows looming in the corners of the room like specters of doubt.

"Tachelle, I need you to understand something," Renz began, his voice low and controlled. "My world is not always glamorous. There are things you might not like, but you have to trust me."

Mahogany, sensing the shift in atmosphere, felt a knot tighten in her stomach. The symbolic elements of their relationship, once glittering like diamonds, now mirrored her internal conflict. She looked into Renz's eyes, searching for the man she had fallen for amidst the complexities of his world.

As the days passed, Renz's violent tendencies emerged more prominently. Mahogany witnessed heated arguments, slammed doors, and glimpses of a side she never thought existed. The shadows of love and deceit danced on the edges of their seemingly perfect life, casting doubts and insecurities into the glittering darkness of their surroundings.

Amid the luxurious trappings of their penthouse, Mahogany grappled with the realization that Renz's world was more complex and volatile than she had ever imagined. The subplot of her internal conflict became a silent undercurrent, mirroring the turbulence beneath the surface of their relationship.

The neon lights of Velvet Dreams seemed a distant memory as Mahogany navigated the shadows of love and deceit. The club's nocturnal tales mirrored her own, and the whispers of desire now intertwined with the echoes of tension that reverberated through their lives.

In the heart of Atlanta's dazzling lights, Mahogany faced a choice – to confront the shadows that threatened her fairy tale or to continue dancing in the neon glow, blinded by the allure of love and luxury.

MAHOGANY'S LIFE WITH Renz unfolded in a whirlwind of luxury and desire, but shadows began to creep into the corners of her fairy-tale romance. The neon glow of Velvet Dreams couldn't shield her from the darker aspects of Renz's world.

Tachelle, now fully immersed in her new identity as Mahogany, reveled in the opulence that Renz provided. The lavish penthouse, adorned with decadence, served as a backdrop to their escalating relationship. Yet, subtle moments of tension seeped in like cracks forming in the facade of their perfect love story.

One evening, as they shared a quiet moment in their expansive living room, a sudden change in Renz's demeanor caught Mahogany off guard. The soft whispers of love were replaced by an unsettling silence, shadows looming in the corners of the room like specters of doubt.

"Tachelle, I need you to understand something," Renz began, his voice low and controlled. "My world is not always glamorous. There are things you might not like, but you have to trust me."

Mahogany, sensing the shift in atmosphere, felt a knot tighten in her stomach. The symbolic elements of their relationship, once glittering like diamonds, now mirrored her internal conflict. She looked into Renz's eyes, searching for the man she had fallen for amidst the complexities of his world.

As the days passed, Renz's violent tendencies emerged more prominently. Mahogany witnessed heated arguments, slammed doors, and glimpses of a side she never thought existed. The shadows of love and deceit danced on the edges of their seemingly perfect life, casting doubts and insecurities into the glittering darkness of their surroundings.

Amid the luxurious trappings of their penthouse, Mahogany grappled with the realization that Renz's world was more complex and volatile than she had ever imagined. The subplot of her internal conflict became a silent undercurrent, mirroring the turbulence beneath the surface of their relationship.

The neon lights of Velvet Dreams seemed a distant memory as Mahogany navigated the shadows of love and deceit. The club's nocturnal tales mirrored her own, and the whispers of desire now intertwined with the echoes of tension that reverberated through their lives.

In the heart of Atlanta's dazzling lights, Mahogany faced a choice – to confront the shadows that threatened her fairy tale or to continue dancing in the neon glow, blinded by the allure of love and luxury.

ONE EVENING, THE TENSION reached a breaking point. Renz had come home late, the smell of whiskey clinging to him like a shadow. Mahogany sat on the edge of their king-sized bed, worry etched into her features.

"Renz, where have you been? I was worried," she began, her voice trembling with a mix of concern and frustration.

Renz shrugged off his jacket, his movements slow and deliberate. "Business, Mah. It's always business."

"But it's more than that, isn't it?" Mahogany's eyes pleaded for honesty. "The late nights, the bruises you try to hide. What's really going on, Renz?"

Renz's eyes flashed with a mix of anger and desperation. "You wouldn't understand. It's not your world."

"Make me understand," Mahogany implored, stepping closer. "I want to be there for you, but I can't if you shut me out."

Renz sighed heavily, the weight of his secrets pressing down on him. "It's dangerous, Mah. The people I deal with... it's not a game."

Mahogany reached out, her fingers brushing against his cheek. "I don't care about the danger. I care about you. We can face this together."

For a moment, Renz softened, his eyes meeting hers with a flicker of vulnerability. "I'm trying to protect you," he whispered, his voice cracking. "But sometimes, the shadows are too deep."

As the weeks unfolded, Mahogany's internal conflict grew. The lavish gifts and declarations of love felt hollow against the backdrop of Renz's violent world. She found herself questioning the foundation of their relationship, wondering if love could truly conquer the darkness.

ONE NIGHT, AS THE NEON lights flickered outside their window, Mahogany stood at the balcony, the city sprawled out before her like a sea of lights. Renz joined her, his presence a comforting weight.

"Do you ever think about a different life?" Mahogany asked softly, her eyes fixed on the horizon.

Renz wrapped his arms around her, his chin resting on her shoulder. "Sometimes," he admitted. "But this is the life I chose. And if

Renz cupped her face in his hands, his touch gentle yet firm. "We can find a way, Mah. Together, we can face anything."

Mahogany leaned into his touch, the warmth of his hands a fleeting comfort against the chill of uncertainty. "Promise me, Renz. Promise me we'll find a way out of the shadows."

"I promise," Renz whispered, sealing his vow with a kiss.

AS THE NIGHT PRESSED on, Mahogany and Renz retreated to their bed, the whispers of love and deceit mingling in the darkness. The neon lights of Velvet Dreams continued to dance in the distance, a reminder of the world they both navigated.

Mahogany lay awake, her mind a whirlwind of thoughts. The shadows of love and deceit were ever-present, but she clung to the hope that they could find a way to the light.

In the heart of Atlanta, amid the dazzling lights and hidden dangers, Mahogany and Renz's love story continued to unfold. It was a tale of passion and power, of light and shadow, and of a love that refused to be extinguished.

Chapter 8: Debts in the Shadows

The opulence of Mahogany's life with Renz masked a growing undercurrent of danger. The whispers of love and deceit intertwined with a new, more menacing force: the looming threat of the Russian Mob. Renz's world was far more perilous than Mahogany had ever imagined, and the shadows were closing in fast.

One evening, as the neon lights of Velvet Dreams cast their hypnotic glow, Renz sat in his office, the weight of his debts pressing heavily on his mind. His business dealings, once shrouded in glamour, now felt like a ticking time bomb.

Mahogany, sensing his unease, approached him. "Renz, what's wrong? You've been distant."

Renz glanced at her, his eyes filled with a mixture of love and worry. "It's nothing, Mah. Just business."

But Mahogany wasn't convinced. She knew Renz too well. "It's more than that. Talk to me."

Renz sighed, running a hand through his hair. "There are things I can't tell you. Not because I don't want to, but because I need to protect you."

Before Mahogany could press further, the door to Renz's office burst open. Two burly men, their presence exuding menace, stepped inside. Their sharp features and cold eyes immediately set Mahogany on edge.

"Renz Ivanovich," one of them began, his voice thick with a Russian accent. "We have business to discuss."

Mahogany's heart raced as she realized the gravity of the situation. She looked at Renz, who had turned pale, his confident demeanor replaced by a look of dread.

"Mah, go to the bedroom," Renz ordered, his voice trembling slightly. "Now."

Reluctantly, Mahogany obeyed, but she kept the door ajar, her curiosity and concern overpowering her fear.

The taller of the two men stepped forward, grabbing Renz by the collar and slamming him against the wall. "You owe us $200,000, Renz. The boss is getting impatient."

Renz struggled to maintain his composure. "I'll get the money. I just need more time."

The second man, a scar running down his cheek, chuckled darkly. "Time is a luxury you don't have. You have 40 days to pay up, or things will get very unpleasant."

Mahogany watched in horror as the men roughed up Renz, their fists connecting with his body with sickening thuds. Blood trickled from Renz's mouth, and he groaned in pain, but his eyes remained defiant.

The taller man leaned in, his voice a menacing whisper. "Remember, Renz. Forty days. Or your pretty little girlfriend might find herself in a world of hurt."

With that, the men released Renz, letting him slump to the floor. They left as abruptly as they had arrived, the door slamming shut behind them. Mahogany rushed to Renz's side, her hands trembling as she helped him up.

"Renz, what have you gotten yourself into?" she whispered, her voice breaking.

Renz wiped the blood from his mouth, his eyes filled with a mixture of pain and determination. "It's the Russian Mob, Mah. I owe them $200,000. I thought I could handle it, but..."

Mahogany's mind raced. The shadows of Renz's world had now fully enveloped them. "We need to figure this out, Renz. We can't let them destroy us."

Renz nodded, his resolve hardening. "We'll find a way, Mah. I promise."

THE DAYS THAT FOLLOWED were a blur of tension and fear. Renz scrambled to gather the money, tapping into every resource he had. Mahogany stood by him, her love and loyalty unwavering, but the fear of the looming deadline gnawed at her.

At Velvet Dreams, the usual glitz and glamour felt tainted by the shadows of their predicament. Mahogany performed each night, her mind distracted by the threats that loomed over them. Renz's presence at the club became more guarded, his eyes constantly scanning for any signs of danger.

One night, after a particularly electrifying performance, Mahogany found Renz in his office, staring at a pile of paperwork with a look of despair.

"Renz, we need to talk," she said, closing the door behind her.

Renz looked up, exhaustion etched into his features. "Mah, I don't know how we're going to do this. The money... it's just not coming together."

Mahogany sat beside him, taking his hand in hers. "We have to think outside the box. Maybe there's another way."

Renz shook his head. "The Mob doesn't take IOUs or promises. They want cash, and they want it now."

A thought struck Mahogany, and she hesitated before voicing it. "What if we sold some of the assets? The penthouse, the cars... anything that could get us closer to the amount."

Renz frowned, considering her suggestion. "It might work, but it won't be enough. We need to find a big score, something that will cover the debt in one go."

Mahogany's mind raced, trying to think of a solution. The stakes were higher than ever, and failure was not an option. She squeezed Renz's hand, determination shining in her eyes. "We'll figure it out, Renz. We have to."

THE DAYS CONTINUED to slip away, each one bringing them closer to the deadline. Renz and Mahogany worked tirelessly, exploring every possible avenue to raise the money. The stress took its toll, but their love remained a beacon of hope in the encroaching darkness.

As the 40-day deadline loomed, Mahogany knew they were running out of time. The shadows of the Russian Mob hung over them like a dark cloud, threatening to shatter the life they had built together.

One evening, as they sat in their penthouse, Mahogany looked at Renz, her heart aching with love and fear. "No matter what happens, Renz, we'll face it together. I won't let them tear us apart."

Renz pulled her close, their foreheads touching. "I love you, Mah. And I promise you, we'll find a way out of this. Together."

The neon lights of the city flickered outside, casting their glow into the room. In that moment, Mahogany and Renz held onto each other their love a fragile yet unbreakable bond against the shadows that threatened to consume them.

Chapter 9: Get It How You Live

The neon lights of Atlanta flickered like distant memories, casting a restless glow over the city streets. Renz paced in his penthouse, the weight of his predicament pressing heavily on his shoulders. The deadline for the $200,000 debt loomed ever closer, and he knew he needed a miracle.

A knock on the door broke his reverie. Mahogany answered it, revealing a figure from Renz's past. Smoke, his childhood best friend, stood in the doorway, fresh out of a six-year prison stint for aggravated assault. His eyes, hardened by the years behind bars, softened slightly as they met Renz's.

"Renz, my man," Smoke greeted, pulling Renz into a tight embrace. "It's been too long."

"Too long, indeed," Renz replied, his voice strained with the burden of his troubles. "Let's talk."

They sat in the dimly lit living room, the city's nocturnal hum a backdrop to their conversation. Renz recounted the events that had led him to this desperate point, sparing no detail about his debt to the Russian Mob and the brutal beating he had received.

Smoke listened intently, his expression growing more serious with each word. "So, you need $200,000 in less than forty days," he summarized, his mind already racing with possibilities. "And you're willing to do whatever it takes to get it."

"Anything," Renz confirmed, his voice steady. "I can't let them hurt Mahogany. We need to get this money, Smoke. Any means necessary."

Smoke nodded, a sly smile forming on his lips. "Well, then. Let's get it how we live."

THE FOLLOWING DAYS were a whirlwind of planning and action. Smoke's experience on the streets and his time in prison had given him a ruthless edge, and Renz, driven by desperation, followed his lead.

Their first target was a high-stakes poker game held in the basement of a luxurious mansion in Buckhead. Smoke, with his streetwise charm, bluffed his way into the game while Renz acted as a lookout. The room was thick with cigar smoke and the sound of chips clinking against each other.

As Smoke sat down at the poker table, he flashed a confident smile at the other players. "Hope y'all ready to lose some money," he joked, his voice dripping with casual bravado.

The other players chuckled, underestimating him as a novice. Smoke played the part perfectly, losing small amounts at first, then striking with a calculated finesse. He watched each player's habits, noting who bluffed and who folded easily.

"Raise to five thousand," Smoke announced during a pivotal hand, pushing a stack of chips forward.

One of the other players, a heavyset man with a gold watch, sneered. "Big move for a newbie. You sure you can handle it?"

Smoke leaned back, his eyes glinting with amusement. "Guess we'll find out."

The man called his bluff, and when the cards were revealed, Smoke's straight flush beat the man's three of a kind. The room erupted in murmurs as Smoke raked in the chips, his expression never wavering.

By the end of the night, they walked away with nearly $20,000.

"One down," Smoke said, pocketing the cash. "A lot more to go."

THEIR NEXT HEIST TOOK them to a jewelry store on Peachtree Street. Posing as affluent buyers, they scoped out the store, noting the positions of the cameras and the habits of the staff. One rainy afternoon, when the store was nearly empty, they struck.

Renz and Smoke entered the store, their appearances slick and polished. Renz engaged the store manager, a middle-aged woman with a discerning eye, in a conversation about custom engagement rings.

"This one right here," Renz said, pointing to a diamond-studded band. "How much would it set me back?"

The manager smiled, pulling out the ring for closer inspection. "That's one of our finest pieces. It's priced at fifty thousand dollars."

As she handed the ring to Renz, Smoke moved to the display cases, his eyes scanning for high-value targets. He noted the security cameras' blind spots and the routine movements of the staff.

Suddenly, Renz staged a loud argument with a supposed accomplice who had just entered the store. "What do you mean you don't have the money?" Renz shouted, drawing everyone's attention.

As the staff rushed to calm the situation, Smoke slipped behind the counter, his movements fluid and precise. He filled his bag with diamonds and gold, each piece glittering under the store's fluorescent lights.

In the chaos, they slipped out unnoticed, their hearts pounding with the thrill of the successful heist. They had netted another $50,000 worth of jewels, which they quickly fenced through Smoke's contacts.

THEIR FINAL SCHEME was the most dangerous. They targeted a local drug dealer known for his extravagant lifestyle and loose security. Under the cover of night, they broke into his safe house, the dim glow of streetlights casting long shadows as they moved silently through the house.

The encounter was tense. They found the dealer asleep, a gun under his pillow. With practiced efficiency, Smoke disarmed him and tied him up while Renz located the safe.

The dealer woke with a start, his eyes widening in fear. "What the hell? Who are you?" he demanded, struggling against the ropes.

"Doesn't matter," Smoke replied coldly. "Just tell us the combination."

"Go to hell," the dealer spat.

Smoke's patience snapped. He grabbed the dealer by the collar, his face inches away. "Tell us the combination, or I swear you'll regret it."

Seeing the deadly seriousness in Smoke's eyes, the dealer relented. "Fine, fine! It's 17-24-36."

Renz opened the safe, revealing stacks of cash and drugs. "Jackpot," he whispered, his eyes gleaming with triumph. They gathered everything they could carry, leaving the dealer bound but unharmed.

BACK AT THE PENTHOUSE, Renz and Smoke counted their spoils. The total was impressive, but still not quite enough to meet the $200,000 mark. They were close, but not close enough.

Renz's phone buzzed, and he saw a text from Mahogany: "Be careful. I love you."

He looked at Smoke, his resolve hardening. "One more job. Just one more, and we're out."

Smoke nodded. "Let's make it count."

The neon lights of Atlanta shone brightly, casting long shadows as Renz and Smoke prepared for their final heist. The city was their playground, and they would stop at nothing to secure their future.

Together, they stepped into the night, driven by desperation, loyalty, and the unyielding need to survive.

The tension in the air was palpable as Renz and Smoke plotted their next move, but back at Velvet Dreams, Mahogany was grappling with her own fears. She knew the dangers Renz was facing, and it weighed heavily on her heart. The club's seductive lights and the rhythmic beats of the music did little to calm her nerves.

One night, after her performance, Mahogany found Zy in the dressing room, applying her makeup. Zy, always perceptive, noticed the worry etched on Mahogany's face.

"What's going on, Mah? You look like you've seen a ghost," Zy said, her voice gentle but firm.

Mahogany sighed, sitting down beside Zy. "It's Renz. He's in deep trouble with the Russians. He owes them a lot of money, and the deadline is coming up fast."

Zy put down her makeup brush, turning to face Mahogany. "And you're worried about what might happen if he doesn't come up with the money in time."

Mahogany nodded, tears welling up in her eyes. "I can't just sit here and do nothing, Zy. I feel so helpless."

Zy reached out, taking Mahogany's hand in hers. "Then we won't sit around and do nothing. We can come up with our own schemes to help out. We've got skills, Mah. We know how to play this game."

Mahogany looked at her friend, hope sparking in her eyes. "You really think we can make a difference?"

Zy smiled, her eyes gleaming with determination. "I know we can. Let's show these boys how it's done."

THE NEXT NIGHT, ZY and Mahogany put their plan into action. They scouted Velvet Dreams for potential targets, their eyes sharp and calculating. The club was filled with men eager to spend their money, their inhibitions lowered by alcohol and the allure of the performers.

Their first mark was a middle-aged businessman, visibly drunk and throwing money around like it was nothing. Zy approached him with a sultry smile, her body language exuding confidence.

"Hey there, handsome," she purred, sliding into the seat next to him. "Mind buying a girl a drink?"

The man grinned, clearly taken with Zy's charm. "Sure thing, beautiful. What's your name?"

"Zy," she replied, her voice smooth as silk. "And you are?"

"Call me Greg," he said, signaling the bartender. "Get this lady whatever she wants."

As Zy engaged Greg in conversation, Mahogany subtly joined them, her presence adding to the allure. They played their roles perfectly, weaving a web of flirtation and false promises. It wasn't long before Greg was spilling his secrets, boasting about his wealth and business ventures.

"You know, Greg," Mahogany said, leaning in close, "you should let us show you a good time. We know how to make a man feel special."

Greg's eyes lit up with excitement. "I'd like that. What do you have in mind?"

The girls exchanged a knowing glance. "Let's go somewhere private," Zy suggested, her voice dripping with seduction. "We promise it'll be worth your while."

They led Greg to a secluded VIP room, where the real con began. They played him like a fiddle, extracting as much money as they could without him realizing he was being duped. By the end of the night, they had pocketed several thousand dollars.

THEIR SUCCESS EMBOLDENED them, and they continued their schemes night after night, targeting the club's wealthiest and most gullible patrons. Each con was a careful dance of manipulation and deceit, and they executed it flawlessly.

One evening, they set their sights on a young tech entrepreneur named Daniel, who was celebrating a recent business deal. He was flashy, arrogant, and exactly the kind of mark they could exploit.

Zy approached him first, her charm disarming him immediately. "Congratulations on your big win," she said, clinking her glass against his. "You must be feeling on top of the world."

Daniel grinned, his ego inflated by the attention. "Thanks, darling. It's been a great night."

Mahogany joined them, her smile dazzling. "We heard you're quite the success story. How about we make this night even more memorable?"

Daniel, eager to impress, agreed to their suggestion of a private after-party. They led him to a secluded part of the club, where they began their usual routine of sweet talk and seduction.

However, this time things took a dangerous turn. Unbeknownst to the girls, Daniel was more shrewd than he appeared. He had noticed the pattern of their cons and decided to play along to see where it led.

As the night progressed, Daniel's demeanor shifted. "You know," he said, his voice taking on a menacing edge, "I think it's time we had a little talk about what you're really up to."

Mahogany and Zy exchanged a worried glance. "What do you mean?" Mahogany asked, trying to maintain her composure.

Daniel's smile was cold. "You think I'm stupid? I've seen how you two operate. But tonight, you picked the wrong mark."

Before they could react, two burly men emerged from the shadows, grabbing Mahogany and Zy. Panic surged through them as they struggled against the strong grips.

"Let us go!" Zy demanded, her voice shaking.

Daniel stepped closer, his expression devoid of empathy. "Not until we settle this. You tried to play me, and now you're going to pay."

The men dragged Mahogany and Zy toward a waiting car, their hearts pounding with fear. But just as they were forced inside, Mahogany spotted a familiar face in the distance – one of the club's security guards who had always had a soft spot for her.

Desperation fueled her actions. "Help us! Please!" she screamed, her voice echoing through the alley.

The guard's eyes widened as he recognized Mahogany. He rushed over, his hand on his radio. "What's going on here?"

Daniel's henchmen hesitated, unsure of how to handle the situation. The guard pulled out his radio and called for backup, his voice authoritative. "We've got a problem in the alley. Send help now."

Within minutes, more security personnel arrived, forcing Daniel and his men to retreat. Mahogany and Zy were freed, their bodies trembling with adrenaline.

"Thank you," Mahogany gasped, clutching the guard's arm. "You saved us."

The guard nodded, his expression serious. "You girls need to be more careful. This city is dangerous."

As they made their way back into the club, Mahogany and Zy knew they had narrowly escaped a dire fate. The encounter served as a stark reminder of the risks they faced in their desperate quest to save Renz.

THE DAYS CONTINUED to blur into nights, and the pressure mounted as the deadline drew closer. Mahogany and Zy, undeterred by their near-kidnapping, intensified their efforts, driven by the urgent need to secure the money.

Together, they navigated the shadows of Atlanta, tricking and finessing their way through the city's underbelly. Each encounter was a calculated risk, a step further into the treacherous world they had chosen to survive in.

As they worked tirelessly, Renz and Smoke were also making strides, their heists becoming bolder and more lucrative. But time was running out, and the shadow of the Russian Mob loomed ever larger.

In the heart of Atlanta's neon-lit nights, Mahogany, Renz, Zy, and Smoke fought against the odds, their lives intertwined by desperation and loyalty. The city was a dangerous playground, and they would stop at nothing to secure their future, no matter the cost.

The moon hung high in the sky as Renz, Mahogany, Smoke, and Zy stepped out of the sleek black SUV, the night promising a respite from the chaos that had gripped their lives. They had decided to take a break and enjoy a double date at one of Atlanta's upscale restaurants. The city lights glittered around them, casting a hopeful glow on the evening.

Inside, the restaurant was an oasis of elegance. Soft jazz music played in the background, and the warm lighting bathed everything in a golden hue. They settled into a plush booth, ordering drinks and appetizers, laughter and conversation flowing easily.

Renz, feeling a rare moment of relaxation, held Mahogany's hand under the table. Smoke and Zy shared a knowing look, the camaraderie between them as strong as ever.

As the main course arrived, Mahogany glanced nervously at Zy before turning to Renz. "I have something to give you," she said, her voice a mix of excitement and anxiety.

Renz raised an eyebrow, curiosity piqued. "What is it, Mah?"

Mahogany reached into her purse and pulled out a thick envelope, placing it in front of Renz. "Open it," she urged softly.

Renz opened the envelope and stared at the contents. His eyes widened in shock. "Twenty-three thousand dollars?" he said, incredulous. "You made all this dancing?"

Mahogany bit her lip, glancing at Zy for support. "No," she admitted. "It wasn't just me. It was Zy too. We've been making some moves of our own."

Renz's expression hardened. "What kind of moves?"

Mahogany took a deep breath and began to explain their schemes, detailing the cons they had pulled on various patrons at Velvet Dreams. Zy chimed in occasionally, adding details and trying to emphasize that it was all for the greater good.

As Mahogany spoke, Renz's face darkened. The realization that Mahogany had been taking action without his direction or consent gnawed at his insecurities. He clenched his fists under the table, struggling to keep his emotions in check.

When Mahogany finished, Renz's voice was cold and edged with anger. "So you thought it was a good idea to risk your lives running these scams? Without telling me? Without my protection?"

Mahogany's eyes filled with tears. "We were just trying to help, Renz. We knew you needed the money, and we didn't want to just sit around and do nothing."

Zy, sensing the rising tension, interjected. "We handled ourselves just fine, Renz. We're not helpless."

But Renz's insecurities had taken root, and they manifested as anger. He stood up abruptly, towering over the table. "This isn't a game! You put yourselves in danger for what? A few thousand dollars? You think that's worth the risk?"

His voice grew louder, drawing the attention of nearby diners. Smoke tried to calm him down, but Renz was beyond reason. "You," he said, pointing a finger at Zy, "I know you put her up to this. You always have some scheme, don't you? Well, this time, you've gone too far."

Zy bristled at the accusation, but before she could respond, Renz turned back to Mahogany. "And you," he said, his voice breaking slightly, "I can't believe you'd do this without talking to me. I thought we were in this together."

Mahogany's tears spilled over. "We are, Renz. I just wanted to help."

Renz's face softened for a moment, but then he shook his head, the anger returning. "No. This is too dangerous. I can't have you here while things are so volatile. You're going to Miami to stay with my cousin Kendra. You'll be safer there."

Mahogany's heart sank. "But Renz, I want to be here with you."

"No," he said firmly. "You need to go. I'll handle things here with Smoke. You dancing in Miami is the best way to keep you safe."

The table fell into an uneasy silence, the earlier camaraderie shattered by the confrontation. Smoke looked at Zy, worry etched on his face, while Zy glared defiantly at Renz.

As they left the restaurant, the weight of the decision pressed heavily on them all. Mahogany clung to Renz, her heart aching at the thought of leaving him, while Renz struggled to mask his insecurities as protection.

In the cold night air, they stood by the SUV, Renz's arm around Mahogany. "This is for the best," he said quietly, trying to convince himself as much as her.

Mahogany nodded, tears still streaming down her face. "I trust you, Renz. Just promise me you'll be careful."

Renz kissed her forehead. "I will. We'll get through this. I promise."

As the SUV pulled away, taking Mahogany and Zy back to the apartment, Renz and Smoke stood together, the city's lights reflecting in their eyes. The night was far from over, and the stakes had never been higher. They were determined to do whatever it took to protect those they loved, even if it meant risking everything.

Chapter 10: Miami Nights

The sultry air of Miami greeted Mahogany as she stepped off the plane, her heart heavy with the weight of recent events. The vibrant city, with its neon lights and pulsating rhythms, was a stark contrast to the tumultuous atmosphere she had left behind in Atlanta. She pulled her suitcase along the bustling terminal, her thoughts a whirlwind of uncertainty and determination.

Waiting for her was Kendra, Renz's cousin, a statuesque woman with caramel skin and a mane of curly hair that cascaded down her back. She waved enthusiastically, her smile warm and inviting.

"Mahogany! Welcome to Miami!" Kendra exclaimed, enveloping her in a tight hug. "We're gonna have you settled in no time."

Mahogany managed a smile, grateful for Kendra's warmth. "Thank you, Kendra. I'm really glad to be here."

As they drove through the city, Kendra filled the air with chatter, pointing out landmarks and hotspots. "You'll love it here, Mahogany. Miami's got this energy that's just contagious. And Gold Rush? It's the best club in town. You're gonna kill it there."

Mahogany peered out of the window, taking in the palm-lined streets and the vibrant murals that adorned the buildings. The city's heartbeat was a mix of Latin rhythms, hip-hop beats, and the sound of the ocean crashing against the shore. It was a place where dreams were chased under the cover of night.

Kendra's apartment was in a sleek high-rise overlooking the ocean. The view from the balcony was breathtaking, the horizon stretching out endlessly. Mahogany let out a sigh, feeling a sense of calm wash over her.

"You can stay here as long as you need," Kendra said, showing her to a cozy guest room. "We'll get you set up at Gold Rush tomorrow. Tonight, we're hitting the town. You need to see what Miami nights are all about."

That evening, Mahogany found herself in the heart of Miami's nightlife. The streets were alive with music, laughter, and the scent of street food. Kendra led her to a popular rooftop bar, where the city sprawled out below them like a sea of twinkling lights.

As they sipped on mojitos, Mahogany felt a flicker of excitement. The weight of Atlanta's troubles seemed to lift, if only for a moment. Kendra's friends were a lively bunch, and Mahogany found herself laughing and dancing, her worries melting away with each beat of the music.

The next day, Kendra took Mahogany to Gold Rush. The club was a palace of decadence, with gold accents and plush velvet seating. The stage was a glittering platform where performers shone like stars.

Mahogany met the club's manager, a sharp-eyed woman named Carmen. "Kendra's told me a lot about you," Carmen said, looking her up and down. "Let's see what you've got."

When Mahogany took the stage, she felt the familiar rush of adrenaline. The music enveloped her, and she moved with the grace and confidence that had made her a star at Velvet Dreams. The audience was captivated, their cheers echoing in her ears.

Carmen's approval was immediate. "You've got talent, Mahogany. Welcome to Gold Rush."

In the weeks that followed, Mahogany became a rising star at the club. Her performances were electric, and the patrons couldn't get enough of her. She reveled in the attention, the tips pouring in like a tide. The camaraderie among the dancers was strong, and she formed fast friendships with her colleagues, each of them a fierce and talented woman carving out her place in the nightlife.

But even as she thrived, the shadows of her past lingered. She stayed in touch with Renz, their conversations a mix of longing and reassurance. She missed him deeply, but she understood the necessity of her exile.

One night, after a particularly successful performance, Mahogany and Kendra sat on the balcony, the city's lights flickering below. "You've really made a name for yourself here," Kendra said, handing her a glass of wine.

Mahogany nodded, gazing at the horizon. "I had to. I can't just sit around and wait. Renz is out there fighting for us, and I need to do my part too."

Kendra smiled, her eyes filled with pride. "You're stronger than you know, Mahogany. Miami's lucky to have you."

As the night wore on, Mahogany felt a renewed sense of purpose. The neon lights of Miami had become a beacon of hope, guiding her through the darkness. She was determined to succeed, not just for herself, but for Renz, Smoke, and Zy. Their fight was far from over, but in the heart of Miami's vibrant nightlife, Mahogany found the strength to keep pushing forward.

AS MAHOGANY DANCED through the neon-lit nights of Miami, the shadows of Renz's world continued to darken. Back in Atlanta, the air was thick with tension, particularly within the confines of a dimly lit office in the back of a nondescript warehouse.

Anatoly Petrov, the feared and enigmatic boss of the Russian mob, sat behind a massive oak desk. The room was suffused with a cold, foreboding silence, broken only by the occasional flicker of the dim overhead light. Petrov's icy blue eyes bore into his associates, his expression one of barely contained impatience.

"Renz," he began, his voice a chilling whisper that demanded attention. "I am growing tired of his excuses. The man owes us two hundred thousand dollars, and we have seen nothing but empty promises and delays."

Boris, a hulking figure with a perpetual scowl etched into his features, nodded in agreement. "Boss, he's been playing us for fools. It's time we remind him who he's dealing with."

Petrov's fingers drummed on the desk, each tap a resounding reminder of his growing frustration. "We need to send a message. Something that will make it clear we are not to be trifled with. We need to hit him where it hurts."

A murmur of agreement rippled through the room. Igor, a wiry man with a predatory gleam in his eyes, leaned forward. "His woman," he suggested. "The dancer. Mahogany. She's in Miami now, right? We could make an example of her."

Petrov's eyes narrowed. "No. Not yet. I want to see Renz squirm first. We go for something closer. His operations, his people."

Boris grunted in approval. "His friend, Smoke. He's fresh out of prison and already up to no good with Renz. We hit him, and we hit him hard."

Petrov nodded, a cold smile playing on his lips. "Yes. Smoke. He's the key. Make sure Renz understands the consequences of defying us."

Igor's smile mirrored Petrov's. "Consider it done, Boss."

MEANWHILE, IN THE VIBRANT heart of Miami, Mahogany was flourishing. Her performances at Gold Rush were nothing short of spectacular, and she had quickly become a sensation. The patrons adored her, and the tips flowed like water.

One night, after a particularly electrifying performance, she was in the dressing room with Kendra, their laughter echoing against the mirrored walls.

"You're a star, Mahogany," Kendra said, handing her a bottle of water. "I've never seen anyone command the stage like you do."

Mahogany smiled, feeling a rush of pride. "It feels good to be doing something I love. And it helps keep my mind off everything back in Atlanta."

Kendra nodded, her expression turning serious. "Have you heard from Renz?"

"Not in the last couple of days," Mahogany admitted. "I know he's got a lot on his plate, but I worry."

Kendra placed a reassuring hand on her shoulder. "He's a fighter. He'll pull through."

Mahogany sighed, hoping Kendra was right. She glanced at her reflection in the mirror, seeing not just the glamorous dancer she had become, but also the resilient woman determined to stand by her man.

BACK IN ATLANTA, RENZ and Smoke were deep in the throes of their latest scheme. The night was cloaked in darkness, the alleyways and side streets providing the perfect cover for their illicit activities.

Smoke, ever the pragmatist, was counting the money from their latest heist, his eyes glinting with satisfaction. "We're getting there, Renz. Another few jobs like this, and we'll have enough to pay off Petrov."

Renz nodded, though his mind was elsewhere. The fear of retribution from the Russian mob was a constant, gnawing worry. "We need to be careful, Smoke. One wrong move, and we're dead."

Smoke clapped him on the back. "Relax, man. We've got this. Just keep your head in the game."

But as they navigated the treacherous path of their criminal endeavors, Petrov's henchmen were already closing in. The attack came swiftly, in the dead of night, as Renz and Smoke were counting their ill-gotten gains in an abandoned warehouse.

The door burst open with a violent crash, and Boris, flanked by a cadre of armed men, stormed in. Renz barely had time to react before a brutal punch to the gut sent him sprawling. Smoke fought back, his fists flying, but the sheer number of assailants overwhelmed him.

Igor stood over Renz, a cruel smile on his lips. "Boss sends his regards."

Renz's vision blurred as he tried to rise, only to be met with a savage kick to the ribs. The pain was excruciating, but the realization that this was only the beginning was far worse.

AS MAHOGANY SETTLED into the rhythm of Miami nights, she remained blissfully unaware of the storm brewing back in Atlanta. Her performances at Gold Rush continued to captivate, each night bringing new faces and new opportunities.

But the shadows of Renz's world loomed ever larger, a silent reminder that the past was never truly left behind. And as the neon lights of Miami flickered in the night, Mahogany danced on, her heart filled with hope and a determination to keep pushing forward, no matter the cost.

THE ASSAULT ON RENZ and Smoke left Renz seething with rage. His body ached from the bruises, but it was the blow to his pride that hurt the most. He couldn't let Petrov get away with this. Sitting in his darkened apartment, he dialed Petrov's number, his hands trembling with fury.

The line clicked, and Petrov's cold, detached voice answered. "Da?"

"You bastard!" Renz shouted, his voice echoing off the walls. "You think you can send your goons to jump me and get away with it? You've got another thing coming!"

A brief silence followed before Petrov responded, his tone chillingly calm. "Renz, you owe a debt. This is a consequence of your failure to pay. Consider it a reminder."

"A reminder?" Renz spat. "You're gonna regret this, Petrov. I'll make sure of it."

"Enough," Petrov interrupted, his voice sharp and authoritative. "The gloves are off, Renz. You have 40 days left. Fail again, and it won't be just a beating next time."

Renz's hand clenched around the phone, veins bulging in his neck. "This isn't over, Petrov. You hear me?"

The call ended abruptly, leaving Renz simmering in silence. He threw the phone across the room, watching as it shattered against the wall. The rage in his chest burned hotter, knowing that the clock was ticking.

MEANWHILE, IN MIAMI, Mahogany was settling into her new life. The vibrant city, with its pulsing nightlife and stunning beaches, offered a stark contrast to the tense atmosphere she had left behind in Atlanta. She had quickly made a name for herself at Gold Rush, her performances drawing in crowds night after night.

One evening, as she lounged by the pool at her hotel, her phone buzzed with a text from Zy.

"In Miami. Can we meet?"

Excitement surged through Mahogany as she texted back the address of her hotel. She had missed her friend and was eager to catch up.

Later that evening, Zy arrived. The two women embraced, and Mahogany felt a wave of relief wash over her.

"It's so good to see you, Zy," Mahogany said, smiling warmly. "How's everything back at Velvet Dreams?"

Zy shrugged, a shadow crossing her face. "It's been rough. With everything going on with Renz and the Russians, the atmosphere is tense. Charmz sends his regards, by the way. He's worried about you."

Mahogany nodded, her heart aching a little at the mention of her old life. "I miss everyone. But I've been doing well here. Let me show you around."

They spent the next few hours exploring the bustling streets of Miami. The neon lights cast a vibrant glow over their adventures, and the sound of laughter filled the air as they caught up on each other's lives.

Eventually, they made their way to Gold Rush, where Mahogany introduced Zy to Kendra and the other dancers. The club was alive with energy, the music thumping and the crowd cheering as Mahogany performed. Zy watched with admiration, impressed by her friend's rising star status.

After the show, they headed back to Mahogany's hotel room, both women feeling the weight of the night's excitement. As Mahogany poured them drinks, Zy stepped out to make a phone call, her voice hushed as she spoke in the hallway.

Mahogany sat on the edge of her bed, reflecting on the whirlwind of the past few weeks. Her thoughts were interrupted by the sudden, jarring sound of glass shattering. She barely had time to react before the room was lit up with the flash of automatic gunfire.

The flash of gunfire was blinding, the cacophony of bullets deafening. Mahogany hit the floor, but not quickly enough. Pain exploded in her side as a bullet tore through her, the force of it knocking the breath out of her lungs. She tried to move, but the world spun, and darkness began to close in around her.

Zy's screams were the last thing she heard before she lost consciousness.

Outside, Zy screamed and ducked for cover, her phone clattering to the floor. The attack seemed to last an eternity before the gunfire finally ceased, leaving an eerie silence in its wake.

Zy burst back into the room, her eyes wide with fear. "Mahogany! Are you okay?"

Mahogany struggled to speak as blood flowed through her mouth and from her head. "Z..Zy!" she rasped.

Zy's face was pale, her hands trembling. "I don't know what to do! Mah! Mahogany!" She cried shaking Mahogany's form as she went unconscious.

Zy grabbed what She could and fled the hotel, the sirens growing louder as they disappeared into the chaotic Miami night. The message from Petrov had been clear: no one was safe, and the gloves were truly off.

In Atlanta, Renz was pacing his apartment, his mind racing with thoughts of retaliation and fear for Mahogany's safety. The sudden ringing of his phone startled him. He grabbed it, praying for good news.

"Hello?"

"Mr. Renz?" The voice on the other end was calm, professional. "This is Dr. Wilson from Miami General. Your partner, Mahogany, has been admitted. She's in critical condition."

Renz's heart stopped. "What? What happened?"

"There was a shooting. She's been hit multiple times and is currently in the ICU. She's in a coma."

The phone slipped from Renz's hand, and he crumpled to the floor, his body wracked with sobs. The weight of the news crushed him, each breath a struggle.

Smoke found him like that, curled up on the floor, his face wet with tears. "What happened, man?"

Renz choked out the words. "Mahogany...she's been shot. She's in a coma."

The two men sat in silence, the gravity of the situation settling over them like a shroud. The quiet was shattered by the sudden ringing of Renz's phone again. He snatched it up, his hand shaking.

"You think the shit with your little slut bucket was something?" The voice on the other end was cold, taunting. "Wait till you see what we do to what you really love."

Renz's blood ran cold. "Who is this?"

The line went dead.

Renz's mind raced. The Russians had made it clear—Mahogany was just the beginning. They would stop at nothing to break him.

"We need to get out of here," Renz said, his voice barely a whisper.

Smoke nodded, his expression grim. "Where to?"

"Anywhere but here. We need to lay low, figure out our next move."

THE DRIVE TO MIAMI was a blur of desperation and fear. Smoke handled the wheel while Renz sat in silence, his mind fixated on Mahogany. He couldn't shake the image of her lying in a hospital bed, fighting for her life because of him.

They arrived at Miami General in the early hours of the morning. The sterile smell of the hospital hit Renz like a punch to the gut as they made their way to the ICU. The sight of Mahogany, pale and still, hooked up to machines, nearly broke him.

He sank into the chair beside her bed, taking her hand in his. "I'm so sorry, Mah. This is all my fault."

Smoke stood guard by the door, his eyes scanning the hallway for any sign of trouble. "We need to keep moving, Renz. It's not safe here."

"I can't leave her," Renz said, his voice cracking. "Not like this."

"You don't have a choice. The Russians know where you are. If we stay, they'll come after you and anyone close to you."

Renz knew Smoke was right. Staying put was a death sentence. He had to keep moving, keep ahead of the danger.

"I'll be back, Mah," he whispered, pressing a kiss to her hand. "I promise."

BACK IN ATLANTA, THE city was already waking up as Renz and Smoke packed their things. The sun was just beginning to rise, casting long shadows across the room.

"We need to disappear," Smoke said, tossing a duffel bag onto the bed. "Find a place to lay low until we can figure out our next move."

Renz nodded, his face set in a grim mask. "I know a place. An old cabin my uncle used to take me to when I was a kid. It's off the grid, out in the middle of nowhere."

Smoke's lips curled into a rare smile. "Perfect. Let's get out of here."

As they left the apartment, Renz cast one last look at the life he was leaving behind. The city that had once been his playground was now a battleground, and the stakes were higher than ever. With Mahogany fighting for her life and the Russians closing in, he knew he had to stay one step ahead.

The road stretched out before them, a long, uncertain journey. But Renz was determined. He would find a way to protect the people he loved, no matter the cost. And when the time was right, he would return to finish what he had started.

Chapter 11: In the Eye of the Storm

Two months had passed, and Mahogany still lay motionless in her hospital bed, suspended in a state between life and death. The gunshot wound to her head had left her in a deep coma, with doctors uncertain of her chances of waking. Her once vibrant world was now reduced to the sterile, beeping confines of the ICU.

Dr. Wilson and a team of specialists were conducting their routine examination. As Dr. Wilson placed the stethoscope against Mahogany's abdomen, his brow furrowed. "That's odd," he muttered.

Dr. Ramirez, a colleague, looked over. "What is it?"

"I think I hear a second heartbeat," Dr. Wilson said, his voice tinged with surprise. "Let's get an ultrasound."

The machine was brought in, and as the image appeared on the screen, the room fell silent. There, nestled within Mahogany's womb, was a tiny life.

"She's four months pregnant," Dr. Wilson announced. "It's a miracle."

IN THE DEPTHS OF HER mind, Mahogany found herself wandering through memories and dreams, a ghostly spectator in her own life. She was back in her childhood home, the scent of magnolias filling the air. She could hear her mother's voice, warm and soothing, singing hymns as she cooked.

"Mahogany," a voice called. She turned to see her younger self, innocent and unburdened by the weight of the world.

"Am I dead?" Mahogany asked, her voice echoing in the empty space.

"No," the younger Mahogany replied. "You're lost. But you can find your way back."

Mahogany thought of Renz, Smoke, and Zy. She worried about them, about the dangers they faced. She felt a pang of guilt for leaving them to fend for themselves. "Are they okay?" she asked.

"They're fighting," the younger Mahogany said. "But they need you. They need your strength."

Mahogany's thoughts turned to her unborn child. "I have a baby," she whispered, her hand drifting to her stomach. "How can I protect it?"

"You have to find your way back," the younger Mahogany urged. "For your baby, for Renz, for yourself."

Mahogany felt a sudden surge of emotion. "What if God has abandoned me?" she asked, her voice trembling. "I've strayed so far from the path my parents raised me on."

"God never abandons His children," the younger Mahogany said, her voice filled with conviction. "No matter how far you wander, He is always there, waiting for you to return."

Mahogany felt tears streaming down her face. "I don't know if I have the strength."

"You do," the younger Mahogany insisted. "You just have to believe."

DR. WILSON STOOD BY Mahogany's bedside, watching her. "She's been through so much," he said softly. "But that baby...it's a sign of hope. We can't give up on her."

IN HER MIND, MAHOGANY found herself standing at a crossroads. One path led back to the life she knew, with all its trials and dangers. The other was shrouded in darkness, leading to an uncertain fate.

"I have to go back," she said, her voice filled with determination. "I have to fight."

She felt a warmth spread through her, like a beacon guiding her home. She took a step forward, and then another, until the darkness began to recede.

IN THE ICU, DR. WILSON noticed a flicker of movement in Mahogany's fingers. "Did you see that?" he exclaimed.

Dr. Ramirez leaned in, her eyes widening. "It's a good sign. She's fighting."

IN HER MIND, MAHOGANY stood at the edge of the darkness, the light growing stronger. She took a deep breath and stepped into the light, her heart filled with hope and determination.

"I'm coming back," she whispered. "For my baby, for Renz, for all of us."

And with that, the shadows began to lift, and Mahogany felt herself being pulled back towards the world of the living, her heart filled with a renewed sense of purpose and faith.

Renz and Smoke found temporary refuge at Renz's father's house in Mobile, Alabama. The house was a modest, weathered structure, nestled in a quiet neighborhood far from the chaos of Atlanta. Here, they had set up a small-time drug ring, their operations slowly gaining traction among the local clientele.

The heat of the Southern sun beat down on them as they worked, bagging up the product and making deliveries. Despite the grueling nature of their new enterprise, the time away from Mahogany gave Renz a chance to reflect on his true inner feelings and the things he had left behind.

One evening, after a particularly busy day, Renz sat on the back porch, nursing a bottle of beer. Smoke joined him, lighting a cigarette and exhaling a cloud of smoke into the humid air.

"We're starting to make some real money here," Smoke said, his voice tinged with excitement. "I've been thinking, maybe we should stay. Build this thing up. We could run Mobile."

Renz shook his head, staring off into the distance. "I can't stay," he said quietly.

Smoke frowned. "Why not? We got a good setup here. It's safe, and we're making bank."

Renz took a long sip of his beer, the liquid cool against the heat of the evening. "There's something more important that Petrov can take from me. Something I can't replace."

Smoke looked at him, understanding dawning in his eyes. "Mahogany."

Renz nodded. "Mahogany. And now, our baby. I found out she's pregnant. I can't leave them unprotected."

Smoke was silent for a moment, then he sighed. "I get it, man. But you gotta understand, going back means facing Petrov head-on. That ain't gonna be pretty."

"I know," Renz said, his voice resolute. "But I can't run forever. I have to face him and settle this debt once and for all."

Smoke took a drag from his cigarette, the tip glowing in the dim light. "Alright. But if we're going back, we need to go back strong. We need a plan."

IN THE QUIET MOMENTS, Renz found himself haunted by memories of the past. Unnamed individuals, precious people he had left behind before meeting Mahogany, surfaced in his thoughts. Their faces were blurred, their names a whisper on the wind, but the pain of their loss was sharp and clear.

He thought about his mother, who had died when he was just a boy, and the friends he had lost to the streets. He remembered the promises he had made to himself, to never let anyone close enough to hurt him again. But Mahogany had broken through his defenses, and now, he couldn't imagine life without her.

The sound of the front door opening interrupted his thoughts. Smoke walked out, his expression serious. "We got a call," he said. "Some guys in Atlanta said they saw Petrov's men looking for us. Word is, they're getting restless."

Renz nodded, his jaw set. "Then we need to move fast. We can't give them any more time."

THE NEXT DAY, RENZ and Smoke made their final preparations. They packed up their supplies, gathered their weapons, and prepared for the journey back to Atlanta. As they loaded the last of their gear into the car, Renz's father came out to see them off.

"Be careful out there," the old man said, his voice gruff with emotion. "And remember, you always got a place here if you need it."

Renz embraced his father, the two men holding onto each other for a moment longer than usual. "Thanks, Pops," Renz said, his voice thick with emotion. "I won't forget."

As they drove away, Renz's thoughts were focused on the road ahead. He knew the dangers that awaited them in Atlanta, but he also knew that he had no choice. He had to face Petrov and settle the debt, not just for himself, but for Mahogany and their unborn child.

The journey was long, the miles stretching out before them like a path of uncertainty. But with each passing hour, Renz's resolve grew stronger. He was ready to face whatever came next, to protect those he loved, and to put an end to the shadows that had haunted him for so long.

MEANWHILE, IN MIAMI, Mahogany remained in a coma, her mind a storm of memories and dreams. Unseen by the doctors and nurses who cared for her, she fought her own battles, struggling to find her way back to the world she had left behind.

In her dreams, she saw Renz, his face lined with worry, his eyes filled with love. She felt the weight of his hand in hers, heard his voice whispering words of comfort and hope. And she knew, deep in her heart, that she had to find her way back to him, to their child, and to the life they were meant to share.

As the days turned into weeks, and the weeks into months, Mahogany continued to fight, her spirit unbroken. And in the quiet moments, when the world outside seemed so far away, she held onto the hope that one day, she would wake up and find herself back in Renz's arms, safe and loved, and ready to face whatever the future held.

Chapter 11: In the Eye of the Storm (Final Section)

The dim light of the motel room cast long shadows on the walls as Zy sat on the bed, counting a large stack of money. The bills slipped through her fingers, the soft rustle of paper the only sound in the room. She had done well for herself, amassing a small fortune from their various schemes, but the weight of extreme regret and guilt pressed down on her chest like a heavy stone.

She paused, staring at the pile of cash before her. It should have felt like a victory, but instead, it felt like a noose tightening around her neck. She took a deep breath, trying to push the gnawing guilt to the back of her mind, but it clung to her, refusing to be ignored.

Her thoughts drifted to Mahogany, lying in a coma in the hospital, and the words they had shared the last time they had seen each other. Mahogany had always been like a sister to her, someone she could confide in and trust. But now, that bond felt tainted by the secrets she was keeping, the actions she had taken that had led them all down this dark path.

Zy's phone buzzed on the nightstand, jolting her from her thoughts. She picked it up, seeing a message from Charm: "Any updates?"

She hesitated, her fingers hovering over the screen. What could she say? That everything was falling apart? That she felt like she was drowning in a sea of her own making? Instead, she typed a simple reply: "No news yet. I'll keep you posted."

She set the phone down and stood up, pacing the room. Her mind was a whirlwind of memories and regrets, each one sharper than the last. She thought back to the night of the shooting, the way Mahogany had looked at her with such trust and faith, and how she had failed her friend.

The guilt was like a poison, spreading through her veins and clouding her thoughts. She knew she had to do something, to find a way to make things right, but the path ahead seemed shrouded in darkness.

As she paced, her eyes fell on a small photograph on the nightstand. It was a picture of her and Mahogany, taken during one of their many nights out at Velvet Dreams. They were both smiling, their faces lit up with the joy and freedom of the moment. But now, that happiness seemed like a distant memory, overshadowed by the events that had followed.

Zy sat back down on the bed, picking up the photograph and tracing her fingers over Mahogany's face. "I'm so sorry," she whispered, her voice breaking. "I never meant for any of this to happen."

The weight of her guilt was almost unbearable, but she knew she had to keep going, to find a way to fix what she had broken. She owed it to Mahogany, to Renz, and to herself.

Taking a deep breath, she wiped away her tears and began to formulate a plan. She couldn't undo the past, but she could try to make things right. It was a long shot, but it was the only chance she had.

Zy picked up her phone again, this time dialing a number she hadn't called in a long time. As the phone rang, she steeled herself for the conversation ahead, knowing that it could be the key to turning things around.

"Hello?" a voice answered on the other end.

"It's Zy," she said, her voice firm. "I need your help. It's about Mahogany."

The conversation that followed was tense and filled with uncertainty, but it was a step in the right direction. Zy knew that she couldn't change the past, but she was determined to fight for the future, for Mahogany, and for the life they all deserved.

As the call ended, Zy felt a flicker of hope in her heart. It wasn't much, but it was enough to keep her going. She glanced at the stack of money on the bed, then back at the photograph. There was still a long road ahead, but she was ready to face it, no matter what it took.

With renewed determination, Zy began to pack her things. She had a lot of work to do, and there was no time to waste. The storm was far from over, but she was ready to face it head-on, to fight for the people she loved and to make things right.

And in the quiet moments, when the weight of her guilt threatened to overwhelm her, she held onto the hope that one day, they would all find their way back to each other, stronger and more united than ever before.

Chapter 12: Symphony of Shottas

Moonlight bathed the streets of Miami as Tachelle fought for her life, unaware that Renz, driven by a desperate motivation, orchestrated a plan to sever ties with the Russian mob. Renz and Smoke embarked on their larcenous mission, seeking a solution to the impending threat. Their target: Flip, a former associate now residing in Griffin, Georgia, oblivious to the storm about to descend upon him.

Upon reaching Flip's place of business, the atmosphere shifted. Flip welcomed them, thinking of childhood friendships, not realizing the danger lurking in the shadows. Renz's words hung in the air.

"Renz, my man! Long time no see. What brings you to Griffin?" Flip's smile revealed his easiness.

Renz, his eyes locked on Flip, replied with a sinister edge, "We come bearing gifts!" Showcasing a large Ziploc bag full of money.

Excitement gleamed in Flip's eyes as he rubbed his palms together, "Word, Renz, Smoke! Follow me; let's talk numbers."

Once inside, the trio sat down and caught up on the events of each other's lives over the past few months while sipping on their choice of alcohol, which was brought out and served by Flip's woman, Jasmine, a dark-skinned beauty with big breasts and long legs. "Damn, I thought the nigga was alone. Fuck it, it'll just be two dead bodies instead of one," Renz thought to himself viciously, while subtly cutting his eyes at Smoke, who just nodded in agreement, already knowing his comrade's evil intent.

"So what is the nature of y'all guy's visit? Not to say that it's not both a blessing and a pleasure for us three niggas from the wicked west to chop it up live in the flesh, but we normally conduct our arrangements over the phone. I know y'all ain't trekked way down here to the sticks on a social call. What's the business?" Flip inquired, looking from Smoke to Renz.

"Money, money, and some more muthafuckin' money, my boy. We are in need of some of that dog food you got, about a bird and a half. We also tryna cop a 20-bag bale of some zaa for my luh mans N' dem on the east side," Renz answered, getting straight to it.

Flip looked at Renz questionably before responding, "Nigga, since when did y'all niggas start moving boy? And I thought y'all fucked with the Russian nigga Anatoly. I done tried to drop some work on y'all on more than a few occasions, and y'all always said y'all was straight where y'all was at. Why the sudden change?" He surmised, sounding like the street veteran that he was.

Renz had already anticipated this reaction from Flip, so he had his response ready and automated. "You know, shawty, I've come to understand that life is all about progress. In order to get ahead and proceed to the next level in this shit, you gotta broaden your horizons. To stay stagnant is to die! So let's just say before we were kind of skeptical on the heroin trade, but in light of recent discoveries and a newfound piece of the market, we have decided to plant a seed and watch it flourish. As for Samad, it seems he has fortune 500 executive instead of the sheisty vulture that he really was."

Flip leaned back in his recliner and glanced out of the window for a moment, nodding his head slightly, before returning his attention to the two men sitting across from him. "Spoken like a true scholar of the game, Renz. I'm glad you've come to your senses, and I'll be glad to do business with you, but I must make two things clear first. Yes, y'all niggas are my homeboys; we came up together from free lunch, but I cannot and will not let that affect the funds or the stipulations. My prices will remain the same as I would give anybody else. Business is business. Secondly, if we are to conduct business on this level, it will not be simply a cop and blow type arrangement. Y'all have to be consistent and shop solely with me, and trust and believe not only do I have the best prices on the food that you're likely to find in all of north Georgia, but I guarantee my product is the purest shit on the market as well. So locking in with me is a win/win for both of us, you dig me? Now if y'all are in agreement with that, I'ma give y'all the squares at $45,000 a pop, and fuck a half. Y'all buy one, I'ma throw another in on the face. As far as the weed, I got a couple different flavors. The strongest shit I got now though is some White Pineapple Fruz going for $2200 a 'P,' but if y'all buying ten or better, I'll let it go for $1800. All together that'll be like 80 racks, give or take," Flip explained, running them down thoroughly.

Renz smiled, then nodded his head approvingly while reaching inside his MCM bookbag to retrieve the Ziploc full of currency. "We with you on every point, shawty, and like you already knowing, ain't no pressure on no paper. We got all that and then some right here." He stated factually as he began taking the blocks of money out of the Ziploc and releasing the bills from their rubber band constraints.

Flip returned his smile. "Say less. Lemme go snatch that shit up for y'all boys. I'll be right back," he spoke before turning and exiting the room.

As Flip returned, the tension escalated. Renz and Smoke revealed their true intentions, guns drawn. Flip, caught off guard, was forced to comply, sitting on the floor with hands on his head, while Renz summoned Jasmine.

"Call her down, Flip," Renz demanded, his voice cutting through the room.

Flip, obedient but puzzled, made the call. Unbeknownst to them, Jasmine overheard the whole ordeal while eavesdropping via the house's intercom system. Her heart raced as she dialed 911, threw her phone on the bed, grabbed her pistol, and ran to ride for her man.

In the room, tension thickened. Jasmine descended the stairs, armed with a baby nine-millimeter, the weapon that would later echo in the night.

"Flip, who are these guys?" Jasmine demanded as she entered the room, her small pistol concealed in her hand beside her thigh. The tension was palpable.

Renz, seizing control, snapped, "Bitch! Sit your ass down and shut the fuck up! We're here for the paper, but keep bumpin' ya gums, and we gon' take a few free samples of that fat little twat too! Try me if you want."

Jasmine stared at the gunmen defiantly as the room teetered on the edge of chaos. Just as Smoke made a move to approach her, gunfire erupted. Jasmine, with limited combat experience, upped and recklessly unleashed her Glock, prompting Renz to respond with deadly precision. The room transformed into a battleground, with Flip caught in the crossfire.

Renz, his Glock .17 barking in the chaos, deftly maneuvered, taking cover behind a large wooden chest of drawers. The exchange intensified, but tragedy struck – Smoke fell, a quarter-sized hole in his forehead, leaving Renz momentarily paralyzed by grief.

Regaining focus, Renz pressed forward. Jasmine, outmatched and untrained, fought desperately. In the struggle, Renz silenced her, vengeance coursing through his veins. The back room safe revealed a wealth of money and narcotics – the spoils of a betrayal that stained both the room and his already tainted soul with blood.

Renz, burdened by the weight of his choices, headed for his escape. However, the wailing sirens of approaching police cruisers shattered any hope of a clean getaway. Faced with the inevitable consequences, Renz chose not a life of captivity but a final stand.

In the one-way road's shadows, Renz unleashed a hail of bullets upon the unsuspecting cruisers. The element of surprise favored him initially, but as reinforcements flooded in, Renz retreated behind his suburban, preparing for his final defiant act.

"Nigga, I'm a gangsta! Fuck the law!" Renz yelled, gunfire echoing through the night. As he embraced the inevitability of his fate, Renz, twisted and contorted by hollow tips, acknowledged his journey's dark end. "Damn! I'm going out just like Cleo," he thought, his world fading into an irreversible darkness. The streets of Atlanta, witness to Renz's rise and fall, absorbed the echoes of his tumultuous symphony.

Chapter 13: An Awakening

As the first rays of dawn pierced the Miami skyline, Mahogany stirred in her hospital bed. Monitors beeped rhythmically, a testament to her fragile hold on life. Unbeknownst to her, the same sun that heralded a new day in Miami bore witness to the final, violent moments of Renz's life in Georgia.

In the sterile quiet of her ICU room, Mahogany's fingers twitched, her eyelids fluttering. A nurse, noticing the change, rushed to her side, calling for the doctor. Slowly, agonizingly, Mahogany's eyes opened, unfocused and dazed. She had awakened from her coma.

The doctor entered, his face a mixture of surprise and relief. "Welcome back, Mahogany," he said gently, his voice steadying her in the unfamiliar room. "You've been in a coma for two months."

Mahogany's mind swirled with confusion and pain. She tried to speak, her throat dry and cracked. The nurse brought her water, and with great effort, she managed to ask, "Where... am I?"

"You're in Miami," the doctor explained. "You've been through a lot. It's going to take time to recover, but you're strong. You're going to be okay."

Days blurred into nights as Mahogany re-acclimated to the world around her. Each moment was a painful reminder of her fragility. Physical therapy sessions were grueling. Each step, each stretch was a battle. Her determination was fierce, but her body was weak.

Zy visited often, her presence a comforting reminder of the world outside the hospital walls. On one visit, Zy walked in, her face pale and eyes red from crying. She took a deep breath, trying to steady herself.

"Mahogany, there's something you need to know," Zy said, her voice trembling.

Mahogany's heart pounded. She knew this was not going to be good news. "What is it, Zy?"

Zy sat beside her, taking Mahogany's hand in hers. "Renz and Smoke... they're gone."

Mahogany's world tilted, the room spinning. "What do you mean, gone?"

Zy's tears flowed freely now. "They were killed. Renz and Smoke tried to rob Flip, but things went wrong. There was a shootout. Smoke died instantly, and Renz... Renz didn't make it. He fought till the end, but..."

Mahogany's breath caught in her throat. She felt as if the room had collapsed around her. The love of her life, the father of her unborn child, was gone. She doubled over, a wail of anguish tearing from her lips.

Zy wrapped her arms around Mahogany, holding her tightly. "I'm so sorry, Mahogany. His funeral is next week. I thought you should know."

In the days that followed, Mahogany's recovery took on a different tone. She was no longer just healing from physical wounds; she was grappling with the immense emotional pain of losing Renz. Each step she took, each therapy session, was fueled by a newfound determination – not just to survive, but to seek revenge.

Mahogany's once outgoing and vibrant personality began to fade, replaced by a darker, more reclusive version of herself. She spent long hours staring out of the hospital window, her mind a whirlwind of thoughts and memories.

One evening, as the sun set over the Miami skyline, Zy sat with Mahogany, trying to offer some comfort. "I know this is hard, Mahogany. But you have to stay strong, for yourself and for the baby."

Mahogany's eyes, filled with a steely resolve, met Zy's. "I'm not just going to stay strong, Zy. I'm going to get revenge. Renz didn't deserve to die like that. The people responsible for this... they're going to pay."

Zy hesitated, worry etched on her face. "Mahogany, you need to focus on your recovery. The last thing Renz would want is for you to get hurt."

"I'm not going to get hurt," Mahogany replied, her voice cold and determined. "I'm going to make sure they feel the same pain I do."

In the quiet moments alone, Mahogany's thoughts often drifted to her past. She thought about her parents, her southern Baptist upbringing, and the path she had strayed from. She wondered if God still loved her despite everything she had done. She prayed for strength, for guidance, and for the ability to carry out her plan for revenge.

Mahogany's transformation was palpable. She was no longer the carefree, longing girl she once was. She had become a force to be reckoned with, driven by a singular purpose. The road to recovery was long and painful, but it was fueled by a burning desire for vengeance.

As the days passed, Mahogany's strength grew. She worked tirelessly with her physical therapist, pushing her body to its limits. She was determined to leave the hospital not just as a survivor, but as a warrior ready to avenge the man she loved.

With each passing day, Mahogany's resolve hardened. She knew that the journey ahead would be dangerous, but she was prepared to face whatever came her way. For Renz, for their unborn child, and for herself, she vowed to see justice served.

Mahogany stood in front of the condo she had shared with Renz, a bittersweet sense of nostalgia washing over her. It had been months since she had last been here, and now, standing in the doorway, she felt the weight of his absence more acutely than ever.

The condo was eerily silent as she stepped inside. Memories of laughter, love, and late-night conversations filled the rooms, now hauntingly empty. She walked through the familiar space, running her fingers over the furniture, recalling moments they had shared. But as she explored, she began to realize there was much about Renz she had never known.

In the bedroom, Mahogany was drawn to Renz's closet. She opened the door and was greeted by the sight of his neatly arranged clothes, each piece a testament to his meticulous nature. As she rifled through his belongings, her fingers brushed against a section of the wall that felt different. Curious, she pushed against it and discovered a hidden panel.

Behind the panel was a small safe. Her heart pounded as she knelt down and inspected it. She tried a few combinations, birthdays, and significant dates, but none of them worked. Frustrated, she stood up and continued her search through Renz's things.

It was then that she found it – a diamond-encrusted chain with a heart-shaped pendant. On the back of the pendant was an engraving: "10-05-17." A birthdate? She wasn't sure, but something told her to try it as the combination for the safe.

Her hands shook as she entered the numbers. To her astonishment, the safe clicked open. Inside, Mahogany found stacks of cash, totaling $165,000, a half brick of cocaine, and a couple of pounds of weed. The sight of so much money took her breath away. She thumbed through the bills, feeling a rush of emotions.

Renz had left her a fortune, but he had also left behind a dangerous legacy. As she sat on the floor surrounded by the money, Mahogany felt a pang of longing for Renz. She missed him terribly, but she couldn't help but think about what this newfound wealth could mean for her future.

Yet, along with the wealth came the realization of the life Renz had been leading – a life fraught with danger and secrets. She wondered about the birthdate on the pendant. Whose date of birth was it? Was there someone else in Renz's life she didn't know about?

As the day turned into night, Mahogany sat in the condo, the money spread out before her, deep in thought. The discovery of the safe and its contents had shifted something within her. She was no longer the same woman who had loved Renz unconditionally. She was now a woman who had to navigate a treacherous path, one that could lead to great fortune or deadly consequences.

Her mind wandered to the heart pendant. She held it in her hand, running her thumb over the engraved date. The mystery of it gnawed at her. Who did it belong to? And why had Renz kept it hidden?

With a heavy heart, Mahogany made a silent vow. She would use the money to seek revenge for Renz's death, but she would also uncover the secrets he had kept from her. She would become stronger, smarter, and more ruthless. The love she had for Renz would fuel her determination, but the pain of his loss would sharpen her resolve.

Mahogany knew that the road ahead would be fraught with danger, but she was ready to face it head-on. She would find out who was responsible for Renz's death and make them pay. And she would do it with the same fierce determination that had seen her through her recovery.

As she sat in the dim light of the condo, surrounded by money and memories, Mahogany felt a sense of clarity. She was no longer just a woman grieving her lost love; she was a force to be reckoned with. And she would stop at nothing to avenge Renz and secure her future.

The night deepened, and with it, Mahogany's resolve. She was ready to embrace her new reality and take on the world. She stood up, the diamond pendant glinting in the low light, and walked towards the future, ready for whatever it held.

Chapter 14: Trail of Tears

The day of Renz's funeral arrived with a somber overcast sky that mirrored Mahogany's heavy heart. Dressed in a simple black dress, she felt a mixture of grief and steely resolve. She and Zy arrived at the semi-crowded church, its atmosphere thick with sorrow and a sense of foreboding. The air was filled with the scent of lilies and the soft murmurs of attendees.

As Mahogany took a seat alongside Zy at the back of the church, she scanned the room. Renz's family members were scattered throughout, their faces etched with grief. But what struck her most were the numerous seedy characters from Atlanta's underworld, their presence a stark reminder of the dangerous life Renz had led.

The choir began to sing solemn hymns, their voices rising and falling in a mournful harmony that brought tears to Mahogany's eyes. She clutched Zy's hand, seeking comfort in her friend's presence. The music swirled around them, filling the church with an ethereal sense of peace.

After the final hymn, Reverend Taylor stepped up to the pulpit. His voice, deep and resonant, filled the room as he began to deliver the eulogy. He spoke of Renz's strengths, his flaws, and his undeniable charisma. The words washed over Mahogany, each one a reminder of the man she had loved and lost.

"As we gather here today to remember Lorenzo," Reverend Taylor intoned, "we are reminded of the complexities of life and the people we share it with. Lorenzo was a man who touched many lives in different ways. And now, I would like to invite his widow and the mother of his child to say a few words."

Mahogany felt a jolt of surprise. Widow? Mother of his child? She began to rise, but stopped abruptly when she saw a pretty, slim-framed, light-skinned woman stand from the second row. The woman held the hand of a young boy who bore a striking resemblance to Renz. Mahogany's heart pounded in her chest, disbelief mingling with a sense of dread.

The woman walked to the podium, her presence commanding the attention of everyone in the church. She took the microphone, her voice steady yet filled with emotion. "Hello everybody. To those who might not know me, I am Tamika, Lorenzo's wife."

The words hit Mahogany like a physical blow. She felt the air leave her lungs, her vision blurring as the shock took hold. Beside her, Zy muttered in confusion, "What the fuck!"

Mahogany could barely breathe. The revelation tore through her, each word a dagger to her heart. The man she had loved, the man she thought she knew, had kept such a monumental secret from her. She felt as if the ground had opened up beneath her, swallowing her whole.

Unable to endure the torture any longer, Mahogany stood up abruptly. She pushed past the rows of mourners, her eyes filling with tears. She dashed out of the church, leaving a trail of tears in her wake. The cold air outside hit her face, mingling with her hot tears. She stumbled to the sidewalk, her body wracked with sobs.

Zy followed her, her face a mixture of concern and confusion. "Mahogany, wait!"

But Mahogany couldn't stop. She ran down the street, each step fueled by the pain and betrayal she felt. Her mind was a whirlwind of thoughts – the image of Tamika and the child, Renz's secrets, the life she had imagined and the harsh reality that had just shattered it.

Finally, she collapsed onto a bench, her body shaking with the force of her sobs. Zy caught up to her, wrapping her arms around her friend. "Mahogany, I'm so sorry. I had no idea..."

Mahogany could only shake her head, the words stuck in her throat. She had lost Renz not once, but twice – first to death, and now to the realization that she had never truly known him. The pain was almost too much to bear.

As she sat there, crying on the bench, Mahogany felt something shift inside her. The resolve she had felt earlier that day returned, hardening into something stronger. She would mourn Renz, but she would not let his secrets break her. She would find a way to move forward, to reclaim her life and protect the future that now seemed so uncertain.

The tears continued to fall, but within them was the promise of a new beginning – one born from the ashes of her shattered heart.

The sun hung low in the sky as Mahogany and Zy approached the gates of the cemetery, their steps heavy with sorrow. The journey back to Georgia had been a haze of emotions, the grief and shock of the funeral still fresh in Mahogany's mind. As they entered the cemetery, the soft rustling of leaves and the distant calls of birds provided a haunting soundtrack to their somber task.

Mahogany carried a single white rose, its delicate petals a stark contrast to the darkness that weighed upon her heart. Zy walked beside her, silent but supportive, her presence a comforting anchor in the storm of Mahogany's emotions. They made their way to the freshly dug grave where a simple headstone bore Renz's name.

The funeral had been a torturous experience, revealing secrets that had shattered Mahogany's perception of her relationship with Renz. As she stood at the gravesite, she could still hear Tamika's voice echoing in her mind, each word a reminder of the betrayal and the life Renz had hidden from her.

Mahogany knelt beside the grave, her fingers tracing the engraved letters of Renz's name. Tears welled up in her eyes, but she blinked them back, forcing herself to stay strong. She placed the rose on the grave and took a deep breath, her mind replaying the events that had led her to this moment.

The church had been filled with people she barely recognized, most of them from the darker corners of Atlanta's underworld. Reverend Taylor's words had been comforting at first, but the revelation of Renz's secret life had cast a shadow over the entire service. Seeing Tamika and the child had been a blow, but Mahogany had felt a strange sense of resolve settle over her.

As she looked down at the grave, she whispered, "I will find a way to move on, Renz. I will find a way to live without you, but I will never forget."

Zy placed a hand on Mahogany's shoulder, offering silent support. They stood together in the fading light, the weight of the past heavy on their shoulders. The air was thick with unspoken words and unresolved emotions, but within that silence was a promise of strength and determination.

Mahogany's mind drifted back to the condo she had shared with Renz. Returning there after the funeral had been an emotional journey, each room filled with memories of their life together. She had found the hidden safe behind a false panel in the closet, its contents revealing a side of Renz she had never fully known.

The discovery of the money, drugs, and the diamond-embellished chain had been a stark reminder of the world Renz had inhabited. As she thumbed through the stacks of cash, she couldn't help but feel a mixture of grief and anger. The wealth he had amassed was tainted, a product of the dangerous life that had ultimately led to his death.

Mahogany stood up, brushing the dirt from her knees. "I'm ready to go," she said quietly to Zy.

Zy nodded, and they began the slow walk back to the car. The drive back to the condo was filled with silence, each of them lost in their thoughts. As they entered the condo, the familiar surroundings brought a wave of emotions crashing over Mahogany.

She walked to the living room, where Renz's favorite chair sat empty. She could almost see him there, his laughter filling the room. The memories were bittersweet, each one a reminder of what she had lost.

Zy sat down on the couch, watching Mahogany closely. "You know you don't have to do this alone," she said softly.

Mahogany nodded, her eyes still fixed on the chair. "I know, Zy. But I need to figure out how to move forward. I need to find a way to live without him."

Zy reached out and took Mahogany's hand. "We'll figure it out together. You're not alone in this."

The days that followed were filled with a mix of grief and determination. Mahogany immersed herself in the task of sorting through Renz's belongings, each item a piece of the puzzle that was his life. The more she uncovered, the more she realized how little she had truly known about him.

As she sat in the bedroom, sorting through Renz's clothes, she found a stack of letters hidden in a drawer. The handwriting was unfamiliar, but the words within them revealed a side of Renz she had never seen. The letters were from Tamika, detailing their life together and the child they had shared.

Mahogany's heart ached as she read the letters, the pain of betrayal cutting deep. But within the pain was a resolve to move forward, to find a way to build a new life from the ashes of the old. She knew that the journey ahead would be difficult, but she was determined to find a way.

As the days turned into weeks, Mahogany found herself changing. The outgoing, longing girl she had once been was replaced by a more reclusive and darker version of herself. The betrayal and loss had hardened her, shaping her into someone who could survive in the world that had taken Renz from her. And the pain that he had caused her.

One evening, as she sat alone in the condo, Mahogany made a vow. "I will never again be the victim from here on out I am heartless if it's not my child love is dead to me!"

The vow gave her a sense of purpose, a goal to strive towards in the midst of her grief. As she looked out the window at the city lights, she felt a renewed sense of determination. The path ahead would be difficult, but she was ready to face it, one step at a time.

Chapter 14: Soul On Ice

The neon lights of Velvet Dreams flickered, casting eerie shadows on the walls as Mahogany walked through the club one last time. The familiar scent of perfume and alcohol filled the air, mingling with the low hum of conversations and distant laughter. Her steps echoed in the hallway, a testament to the memories she was leaving behind.

As she made her way to her locker, she was met with familiar faces—friends, coworkers, people who had become like family over the years. But today, she avoided their gazes, her mind focused on the task at hand. She moved through the club like a ghost, her presence barely acknowledged until she encountered Charmz.

He greeted her with a warm hug, his arms wrapping around her in a gesture of comfort and support. Mahogany returned the hug, but Charmz could feel the cold chill emanating from her like an Arctic breeze.

"I know you probably about to say I told you so," she said, her voice tinged with bitterness.

"Nah, Mah, I would never kick you when you're down," Charmz replied softly. "So, where are you headed next?"

Mahogany glanced around cautiously before responding, "What Renz did to me was foul, but what Anatoly Petrov and those fucking Russians did was far worse. They have to pay! I got a hundred thousand and some change, some work and connections. I'm about to head out of town for a while, get all my ducks in a row, then I'm gonna come back and not only take down the Russian mob but take over their territory. I want it all."

Charmz studied her long and hard, searching her eyes for any sign of hesitation. "Tachelle, listen, you didn't come to Atlanta for this. Even though this tragedy has occurred, you are still young. You have your whole life ahead of you. Don't get into this life, Mah," he pleaded.

Mahogany looked him dead in the eyes, her resolve unwavering. "Sometimes when you're in too deep, the only way out is to dig deeper. You take care," she said, pecking him on the cheek and turning to leave.

Before she could reach the door, she heard Charmz call out, "Mah, hold on, wait."

She turned, her expression questioning.

"I'm coming with you," he said, a determined smile on his face.

Mahogany paused, the weight of his words sinking in. A part of her wanted to refuse, to protect him from the path she had chosen. But another part of her, the part that had grown colder and harder, knew she could use the support.

"Are you sure about this, Charmz?" she asked, her voice steady but laced with concern.

"I'm sure," he replied, stepping forward. "Whatever you're planning, you don't have to do it alone."

A small, genuine smile crept across Mahogany's face, a rare glimpse of warmth in her otherwise icy demeanor. Together, they walked out of Velvet Dreams, the neon lights fading into the distance as they stepped into the night.

They loaded into Mahogany's car, the engine purring to life as they pulled away from the club. The road ahead was uncertain, filled with danger and the promise of retribution. But as they drove into the night, Mahogany felt a sense of purpose, a fire that burned brightly within her.

"To be continued..." she whispered to herself, the words a promise of the battle that lay ahead.

As the city lights of Atlanta faded into the rearview mirror, Mahogany and Charmz set off on a journey that would test their limits, push them to the brink, and forge a new destiny from the ashes of the past. The trail of tears they left behind was just the beginning, a prelude to the storm that was about to unfold.

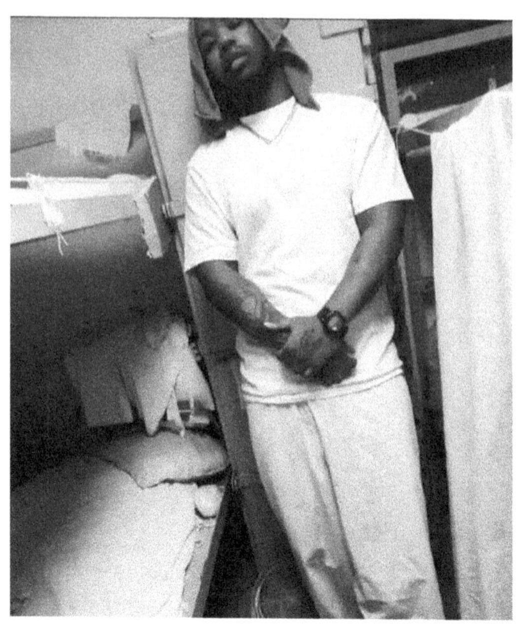

About the Author

James Hardy who goes by the Pen Name "$ENT" is an accomplished author from the Eastside of Atlanta, Georgia. With a unique voice shaped by his personal journey, he has penned the urban novels "The Pain Behind The Pole" and "Beautiful Lies Deadly Deceptions: (A Ghetto Love Affair)," capturing the gritty realities of love, betrayal, and survival. He is also the creative mind behind the heartwarming children's book "Charlie's Incredible Superpower Sandwich."

Currently incarcerated for nearly a decade, James has continued to channel his experiences and imagination into his writing, using his time to reflect and grow as a storyteller. His upcoming release marks the beginning of a new chapter in his life, as he prepares to rejoin society and share more stories that resonate with readers across generations.